Selkirk FC vs the World!

Thomas Clark

Published in 2016 by Selkirk Football Club

A CIP catalogue record for this title is available from the British Library.

For Willie McIlvanney

A View from the Dugout

I've been asked, as is customary, to offer some thoughts ahead of today's big match against The World. This is, of course, the game we have all been waiting for, and the logical conclusion to everything we have been working toward at Selkirk for the last twelve to eighteen months.

First of all, let me please extend a warm welcome to today's visitors to Yarrow Park, i.e. you. In the first half, I hope you will avail yourself of the opportunity to fully explore the many delights which our stadium has to offer, such as the Bob Mercer Memorial Stand, the frighteningly large Garry O'Connor strip which is framed in the Bobby Johnstone Pavilion, and yes, the three different kinds of pies. Also, at some point during the afternoon a football match will be staged.

In the second half, you may find your attention begins to wander. This is perfectly normal. Allow your eyes to lift beyond the VIP decking, the wooden terraces, the tiny dugouts which have caused more head injuries than Duncan Ferguson. Permit yourself the surprise of being surrounded by trees, and the hills, and the beautiful Ettrick Valley. There is a world beyond Selkirk FC, and some of it is even quite pretty.

We hope you enjoy your visit to Yarrow Park. And best wishes, of course, to both sets of supporters; those from Selkirk, and those from everywhere else.

-    Thomas Clark

Table of Contents

Part 1: Selkirk

The Battle o Philiphaugh

The grund appears fae mist, aroon a corner,

The sign ye dinnae spy til ye're upon it,

"Welcome tae Selkirk" - plump blisters o rain

Staun oot like Braille for the blind or unconvertit.

Thare's mair in heaven an earth… That's right enough,

At Yarrow Park, three different kinds o pies,

An Bovril tae! Ower polystyrene cups,

The breaths arise like steam, arise like sighs,

Arise like lofted baws intae the skies,

Arise like lifted herts, like lifted eyes,

Baith baw an breath alike on winter wunds

Are blawn intae the boax, while auld men, wise,

Rememberin, nod their heids fae turtlenecks,

Jut oot tae meet a cross fower decades late,

An Strollers' goalie's, lungin, beaten, fawin…

I'the front row he sees his faither, watchin.

But the Souters gawin mental! Wee Muz, big Gaz,
The Ettrick Valley echoes wi unburdent seats.
Yin pumps his fist at something, runnin past,
A bud o joy amasses I'the sleet,

Then celebrations end. Wi hauns ootstretched,
They peel apairt in blossoms blue and white,
Drift back taewards the line. For nou, thare's time.
Tho the daurk is hairdenin fast. The day turns night.

The baw is waitin. The players, hauns oan waists,
Are lined oan either side, awready ghaists.
The night, alane, the wund will cairy beams
Ower fields whaur ither poets aince dreamt dreams.

The Timin o the Run

Leavin the pub at hauf past two is plenty,

Take in the fine delights

O the river's stroll tae Philiphaugh.

How quiet it is. How the leaf-lined streets

Barely betray a passer-by.

Even when the rugby boys are at hame,

An their grund is dotted wi blue an red,

Whit guilty pleasure! Walkin on by their gate,

Like passin a rival kirk en route tae mass.

An so we dawdle, in oor watch-checkin way,

Pickin up pace as three comes near,

Turnin the corner at the cricket club

An steppin intae Yarrow Park;

An as the ref blaws his whistle

An the captain claps his   hauns,

It's as if the Souters

Have been stood there aw day,

Waitin for you tae show up.

Team Photo: Selkirk, 1946

The war wis ower, it wis a cranreuch day;

The committee men, no sure whaur tae staun

Are dottit aw aroon, lang jaickets an peaked caps,

Watchin the photographer wi jealous eyes.

It's noir like Jimmy Cagney, Alan Ladd,

You couldna ween whit things they've up their sleeves,

Like black marketeers, attemptin tae surmise

Whit price tae pit oan goods that's oan display.

An whit riches! Big men, lined across the bench,

Tryin tae look sma, hunched intae the wind

That shakes the branches, pits hats fae heids,

Drives snell weather in fae fields fae ither launds.

Erms foldit, collars upturnt; their faces are pittit

Wi scars, their mooths wi lines, their eyes wi starin.

Nae sun lies above them, nae shadow below,

Juist the thick black grass, an the absence o licht.

Some Selkirk Haiku

Tap-In

aw o a sudden

withoot his even realisin

the baw at his fit

Cometh the Hour

last meenit corner

anely Phil Addison sees

space at the faur post

Fancy

check oot this fella

thinks he's the bloody ticket

him an his prawn crisps

Ross King

first stairt for Selkirk

"gie it tae the Rangers boy!"

they'll ken his name yet

Loyalty

here

yon wee ginger boy

is he no the wan that usetae play for us

jamie or whitiver his name wis

ye ken the lad

faither usetae come tae games

says he wis lookin for suhin local

an here he is

playin for the fairies

five meenits up the road

thats mair local is it

aw aye

think yer heid buttons up the back

nae loyalty tae onythin

usedtae be

if ye wirnae playin for the souters

ye wirnae playin

an that wis flat

then ye've this clown

five years here an he's niver struck a clean baw yet

och michty me

tellin ye

if they're wantin shot o onybody

there's the man

Take Shelter

It's Scottish Cup day in Selkirk

An aw things are richt;

The redness on the leaves like yon,

The shinin on the watter like yon.

Och, it is a perfect day,

A joke for the guyin o the cynic an the pessimist

Wha woke up sure it would be comin doon;

An no a clood in the sky, nor a drap on the breeze,

Hints at the troubles aheid.

Five Hunner Miles (Away tae Nairn)

The first round draw – they've got the knack

For pickin balls fae oot the sack,

The right yin's warm – click-clack, click-clack,

Or oot the pocket,

Five hunner miles tae Nairn an back?

Ah widnae walk it.

Yer famous for yer toon hall clock,

Yer golfin clubs, yer totey loch,

Yer seaside an yer stocks o rock,

An Tilda Swinton,

Or mebbe that yin's Nairnia. Och,

Whit's the difference?

An as for us, whit's Selkirk got?

Bannocks an battles an history. The lot.

Auld Haining hoose – a lovely spot,

An good for a dauner,

The courthouse o Sir Walter Scott -

Oh, and Garry O'Connor.

Noo, naebody's sayin we'll beat ye easy,

Thae country roads wid make ye queasy;

The boys'll be up bright and breezy,

Doon Yarrow Park,

The macaroni pies are cheesy,

And so's the crack.

But it disnae matter whit ah say,

Us poets yap – we dinnae play,

They'll dae oor talkin on the day,

Set men fae bairn,

The final scoreline – yin, or twae,

But nane for Nairn.

Trainin Nicht

Ceptin the occasional shout

There's nowt but silence;

The thwack o baw on shoe,

A thunder o pursuit.

The trees aroond us,

The deserted road,

The silent river; reverently,

Ah trace the touchline wi ma bit's toe.

Ultras

gretna the ither week there

no much o a gemme

hid the chances like

jist niver goat the breaks

usetae bring a bus or twa did gretna

saw wee wifies noo

grannies giein it

tyke it oop tha field colin

n

rayfaree thet hes to be a fowel

ah mean they wir nice enuff

nae herm in thaim

wantit a wee gab at fuhll time

but ah wisnae in the mood like

no efter that

n onywey

ye cannae unnerstaun a wird thir sayin

Bob Mercer

Bob wis ane o the lucky yins

which is tae say

when he cam back it wis

wi gas in his kist insteid o shrapnel

a tightenin wreath o poison roon his hert

Bob wis ane o the lucky yins

which is tae say

he cam back at aw

led the boys oot bi the watter,

pullt oan the shirt jist ane mair time

Bob wis ane o the lucky yins

which is tae say

it wis anely his freends that died

cut doon on fields at Ypres an the Somme

thair jerseys hingin empty fae the peg

an it wad be poetry tae say

he hung oan in there, or

he waitit until he wis hame

but it widnae be right

senseless at Ettrick Park as onywhaur

that ane death

or ony o them

he just got lucky

but then

Bob was aye ane o the lucky yins

Dyin Breed

thahts you charlie

the doakter sais

baws oan the slates this time

nuhin else wi kin dae

roarn in greetin shi wis

wi didda tell yi

yi daft auld scunner

thahts goat tae be it wi the fitba

tell mi thahts goat tae be it

so ah telt ur it wis

sin thoh caws

ahd a good wee turn oan mi

back in thi day

plaid fir the souters fir a bit

yir da ull mind

bankies wance in the cup

whitta terr thaht wis

hid the fuhll back chasin mi like a skate oan a shoelace

staunin therr up kilbowie park

wi thi baw at ma feet

an thoosans watchin

an davie cooper

an ah says tae um

mon wee man

ah says

mon me n you

wul go fir a walk

Part 2: The World

Scatter My Ashes At Claggan Park

There had been bonfires down at Claggan Park before, plenty of them. Every year when the inspector was due, the entire committee of Fort William F.C. would be there the day before, hauling out from the clubroom cellar great armfuls of rubbish – programmes of games that never happened, musty rolls of scale plans, application forms half filled in. The huge sheets of plastic from the wholesale cans became makeshift dollies for towering heaps of rubble, which were dragged by one corner to the edge of the ground and set alight. The chairman, Alan, used to sit there half the night watching them burn down. Health and safety, he called it, but even when the night winds picked up and blew the bonfire straight like a cape, there was nothing of value within its fiery lick – only the deserted ticket booth, itself stuffed with foul-smelling carpet, and the little chairman on his little chair, his arms hanging limply by his side. Long into the night Alan would sit there in the cold shadow of Ben Nevis, *the mountain with its head in the clouds*, listening to the noxious sizzle of the plastic and the planks of wood popping their red-hot nails. When the caretaker, Dougie, arrived first thing the following morning, the chairman was still there, asleep by a pile of embers. His blazer was spread on his chest like a quilt, and his face was writhing in its dreams.

As their cars pulled in to Claggan Park that day, none of the committee were looking forward to the ceremony with much enthusiasm. They had all gone to the funeral, and the reading of the will, just in case, but they had always found Alan's earnestness deeply depressing, especially now he was dead. It was just like him to have come up with something as daft as this. As they stood around the car park in their various approximations of formal dress, the silence crinkled with the cellophane from fag packets and the snapping of their lighters. When Dougie arrived with the urn buckled in to his passenger seat, they stubbed out their butts on the wooden fence and chucked them into the grass.

Right, let's get this show on the road.

They had briefly thought about just emptying it in the car park, but that was right out. He had been quite specific about it, the nurses said – on the pitch at Claggan Park, right in the centre circle. Auld Ronnie the groundskeeper had been furious. It'd damage the soil, he said. Encourage moles. As they plodded out onto the pitch, there was little reason to believe that the moles needed encouragement.

Great eruptions of dirt piled up everywhere in frothy, cow pat pyramids, leaving giant divots loosely filled with handfuls of sand and soil. The grass had withered badly, and the wind whistled around them as they walked, shivering the distant scaffolds of the goals. The stand, as usual, was empty.

Well, let's get this over with.

When they reached the centre of the pitch, Ronnie, who had insisted on scattering duties, looked around for a suitable patch of grass. The committee members stood with their hands in their pockets, their blue faces chittering with cold. Finally Ronnie found an acceptable spot, a bald patch where little further damage could be done, and started to unscrew the urn's lid.

Anybody want to say a wee word? he asked.

Aye - hurry up, Ronnie, it's freezing.

There were a few half-hearted laughs.

Right yin's in the urn, anyway. If he was here the noo we'd be twenty minutes listening to him.

He meant well, Dougie said.

Finally, the lid was off. Ronnie peered into the open urn like a biscuit tin.

It's there right enough, he said. *Will I just…*

He tilted the urn slowly towards the earth, and shook it. From the black hole, a solid clump of sludge oozed slowly forth and landed on the grass. They stared at it in dismay.

Ronnie, you're meant to chuck it up in the air!

That'll be shining bright! Ronnie snapped. *There's something no right there! I'm no touching it!*

It was true. Something, somewhere had gone badly amiss. The fist-sized lump on the ground looked more like a molten heart than ashes. It trembled slightly as it clung to the fallow grass.

Somebody gonnae get a broom, then?

A few of them murmured uncertainly.

We cannae just sweep him up, someone said. *He was a boring wee fart right enough, but he deserves better than that.*

Murmurs again. A mobile phone buzzed in someone's pocket.

Well, noo whit?

They looked down at it again. It was as solid as ever, though here and there the odd flake unpeeled from it and blew off in the wind.

Look, it's starting to break up a bit. If we leave it overnight, the wind'll sort it oot.

Aye, long as it disnae rain.

They looked up doubtfully at the sky.

Well, there's nae telling. But us standing here's no gonnae change things.

Silently, they began to drift off from the field. With distance creeping in their spirits rose, and they talked about the football, news at other clubs. It was the weekend of the cup final, and most of them had tickets.

Whit aboot it, Dougie? Got yin spare, if you're interested.

Dougie shook his head.

Too much to do here, pal. Enjoy it, though.

One by one the cars all pulled away, reversing from the grass into the car park mud. When the last of them had gone, Dougie swung closed the rusty gate behind them. It hung loose on its only hinge, one of the many long-term projects they'd just never got around to, like the disabled toilets, or the kitchen sink, or the fire safety plan. Aye, it was true enough, Dougie thought. There was a lot still to be done. He picked up a folding chair and walked to the centre circle.

Oh, The Rose!

The village bus was the only one which ran so far out of town, out to where the new stadium was going. It was to be on the verges of things, where the south of Lanarkshire melded unknowably into its north, part of the industrial filler which made separate places contiguous. There had been talk of changing the team's name to reflect this new geographical reality – retaining the Rose, of course, but accommodating by way of acronym or hyphen the other towns on whose outskirts the side would now exist. By such means, they said, could new life be breathed into a club which had long been dying; and indeed, as Ian peered over the wooden blue wall which surrounded the construction area, the concrete swathe could not help but remind him of a cemetery, far removed from the goings-on in town. The scaffold of the main stand was standing upright, though the airy gaps between could still have been filled out with anything, a bottling plant, a shopping mall; and the girders which would support the roof were now bent into place, so that the whole structure was like a half-closed hand emerging from the ground.

It was a cold day, but the rain had already blistered on the grimy trucks and surely would not fall again. There was a burger van, and beside it the remnants of old plastic furniture recovered from who knew what abandoned garden, gleaming white tables cracked in vicious ways and bucket seats lapping with stagnant pools. Ian sat down on the edge of one, lit a cigarette. He tapped his ash into a hole in the table's middle where a parasol once had been. The last of the tan was still fading from his wrists.

Most of the construction workers were young, young enough to be his sons, and he listened to their chatter absently as they took their lunch. They showed each other videos on their mobile phones and laughed, and talked about City and United. The rolls they devoured were flat and white and drooling with onions, dolloped with plastic spoons of sweet brown sauce. Ian squeezed his cigarette between his lips. His eyes were fixed on the trees across the road.

The turn-off was so narrow, and the foliage around it so thick, you could not even tell there was a path until the cars began to emerge. Out they came, in one long continuous line of colour like a magician's handkerchiefs, drawing a gentle hiss from the dewy leaves. Ian waited until they were all gone, then tossed away his cigarette and crossed the road. There was no clear path to walk along up the muddy trail which splayed between the trees. It was wide enough exactly for a car, and there were no sets of footprints anywhere, just two deep trenches of parallel tire marks. Ian squelched up along the side of the track, one arm pushing forward against the branches. There was not much in the way of nourishment here, and the twigs climbed up and over each other toward the flimsiest scraps of light. Little that was living there could be called distinctly this or that, a tree, say, or a bush. It was just growth, unnecessary tangles of root and stump and nettle.

With alarm, Ian realised there was a car trundling out of the clearing just ahead, and he tried to press himself back into the thicket. He was a big man, broad across the shoulders, and had got used to making himself small and manageable. But there was a head poking out of the window of the car, and a hand, and before he could withdraw fully into the trees, a voice called out to him, and he stood still.

"Well, well," the driver said, slowing to a shade short of stopping, "Look who it is! The wanderer returns!"

Ian pinched up the edges of his mouth, approached the car.

"Alright Tommy. How's it going?"

Tommy poked his big square head out of the window.

"Not too shabby. How's things down under?"

Ian ran his tongue along his teeth. They had a sour taste.

"Never worked out."

Tommy scratched his nose. The car was still inching forward, and his other hand was resting on the wheel. Ian watched silently as the bumper of the vehicle approached. There was not enough room on the path for them both, and he stepped back into the mud.

"Is the gaffer about, Tommy, do you know?" he said.

Tommy gestured back towards the clearing with his head.

"Murphy's in the portakabin."

"Nah, no good. It's the boss man I'm needing."

Tommy smiled and shook his head.

"It's me and Murph that's taking things the now. How come?"

No sun had penetrated this far into the wood, and the complacent rumble of the car brought down fusillades of rain from the canopies overhead. Ian felt his trainers taking root amidst the mud.

"You two coaching?" Ian said.

"Aye. Murph's only young, but he knows folk, eh. Knows his stuff."

There was a pause.

"You fixed up yourself?" Tommy asked.

Ian shrugged, ran his thumb around the rim of his nostril.

"Ach, you know. Thistle. Rovers. Nothing I couldn't get out of."

"Coaching?"

"No, playing."

It was only a glance, but Tommy looked at him as if for the first time.

"Oh aye. Good."

The stale rain continued to patter on the car's windscreen, flattening the leaves which stuck to the glass. Tommy sighed and leaned over, turned on the wipers.

"Well, I'll let you get on. Murph's in the portakabin, if you're still wanting him."

Tommy's head retracted into the car, his hand still raised in salute. Ian watched until he passed from view, then walked on up the road. After fifty yards or so, the path terminated in a small gravel carpark, big enough for maybe a dozen decent cars, though only three were left in it now. A portakabin, raised on a scaffold, took up one whole side of the clearing, and a thin row of recently planted willows cut off the gravel from the wide green sweep of the park, where a man in red waterproofs was picking up cones and stacking them beneath his arm. Though it was autumn now, and not yet afternoon, not much of the sky was left.

There was a municipal paddling pool of stone in the park, rarely filled now since it had drowned a child, and some boys were playing barefoot in it, shrieking as they kicked up the miserable spittle of fallen rain and leaves. They were using the pool for a game of cuppie, but the ball kept getting away from them, leaping up between their tackles and skipping exhaustedly onto the grass. Nearby, an old lady sat on a bench and watched the boys with what Ian recognised even without his glasses as absolute disgust, shaking her frizzy head from side to side. As he watched the boys play, Ian leaned his heavy forearm against a sapling, felt it bend. He remembered being back at school, when the Rose had still used the high school's grounds to train, and he had watched them out of the high windows at the back of his classroom. The old railway line had lain uselessly between them, and it had been too far away to make out the details of anything much, and yet those distant smudges had always fascinated him, far more than the very real, very intimate presence of his own teacher. What a waste it had seemed to him, having to sit there and learn about history when all he really wanted to do was to play for the Rose; and there, miraculously, a couple of hundred yards away, the Rose were.

The wind was turning cold again, and the boys had climbed out of the pool, put on their jackets and their shoes. They did not look quite so young anymore. Ian turned away, climbed the stairs of the portakabin quietly.

The office, silent, was raised some three or four feet from out the mud, and a slender runway of planks and piping had been belted around it. The wood on the steps was still white and new, but for the residue of his own feet.

There were two doors on the cabin's front, and the single outward window had been covered with a kind of mesh, so small-bore it was impossible to see through, even if the holes had not been filled with rain. Ian tried to remember what he was going to say, but he couldn't. He lifted his hand towards the nearest door, listened for a moment, lowered himself painfully to one knee. That silence that came from everywhere was dangling in the trees, like a thing that could not break; and through the keyhole he could see nothing, just a small, tremulous world, clear as a marble, with his own pupil in it, watching.

The Keys of Paradise

"Children are the keys of Paradise." – Eric Hoffer

"I'm no going."

"You're going," Euan's mother said firmly, thrusting her arm into a long coat sleeve, "And that's *flat*."

Euan writhed on the couch in agony, his eyes darting around the room for some kind of an alibi. Why couldn't she just go on her own? He went places on his own all the time.

"It's a waste of time. I'm no... I've nae *interest* in it," he burst out desperately. She looked up from tying her jacket belt.

"Oh aye? And whit *are* ye interested in?"

Euan hauled himself upright on the sofa, his eyes glittering.

"Well, listen, right, there's this Hungarian lad coming, name of Bodnar..." His mother sighed loudly.

"Aw, no this again, Euan..."

"Lazlo Bodnar, his name is, from FC Budapest…"

"Is that all you're bothered aboot?" his mother demanded. She was trying to channel outraged surprise, but all she could manage was the outrage. "Swear tae God! The world's going tae hell in a handbasket, looneys running the country, nuclear missiles ten miles up the road, and all *you* care aboot is bloody *Celtic*!" As she said this last part she gave her belt such a violent pull that her top half almost came away from the bottom.

"Aye, but mam, listen, right! Bodnar's signing doon at Parkheid the day, and I'll be just aboot the only one there! They all think he's just another one of these foreign freebies. But me, I've looked him up on Wikipedia and that. I know better!"

"You always do, son," his mother replied, laying her scarf on the back of her neck. Euan's body prickled with remorse.

"Well, I'll *definitely* come tae the next meeting with you, alright?" he said, "I mean, one body either way's no gonnae make much a difference is it?"

Euan's mum shook her head silently, although whether in agreement or disagreement he couldn't tell. As she went through the habitual

48

stations of her departure, checking the plugs, the boiler, the oven, Euan followed close behind.

"This boy Bodnar mam, honestly, he's a prodigy," he gabbled, holding open the door for her, "16 goals in 27 games for Hungary! And I'll be the only one there tae see him sign. I'd kick myself if I missed it!" His mum, having reached the front door, was checking her handbag for her purse. She looked up at him and smiled.

"It's alright, Euan," she said, putting her hand on his head, "You're too young to have to worry aboot all this anyway. It's them that should know better that causes all the trouble, and the young folk that's left to fix it. Just you away and enjoy your fitba."

"I will, ma. Mind the roads, eh."

He watched her down to the foot of the cracked and carless drive, waved goodbye, and closed the door.

***

Life would have been a lot easier for everybody if Euan had just supported Rangers. Ibrox was only two minute's walk from his house, and there were cut-price tickets for locals. It was the standard gesture from clubs like that, a muted apology for the scenes Euan's neighbours opened their curtains to every second Saturday: red-faced men in light blue tops, hordes of them, staggering down the road nine or ten abreast, singing

Hello! Hello! We are the Billy Boys!

We're up tae the knees in Fenian blood,

Surrender or ye'll die!

Euan wasn't entirely sure what a Fenian was, but his dad had been one, by all accounts, and that meant he was one too. That seemed to be the way it worked.

Nobody had really ever explained this stuff to him, and now that his dad was gone, there was nobody left who could. It was a religious thing, he gathered that, but hardly anybody seemed to understand what it was all about. All the folk around here were dirty Bluenoses anyway, whose interest in him extended no further than noting that he was walking the wrong way on matchdays, and whose charity limited itself to blanking the green-and-white fronds that trailed from the scarf in his pocket. *They* weren't about to sit him down and initiate him into the mysteries of things. Every time he made it up to Celtic Park he hoped against all hope that somebody would notice him sitting there, by himself, his threadbare scarf knotted around his hands like rosaries, and take him under their wing; but nobody ever did.

He didn't get over to Celtic Park that often. He could hardly afford the transport, never mind the £40 to get in. As he went down the subway stairs, he checked his pockets repeatedly; keys, ticket, autograph book. Normally these little rituals in crowded places cost him a thump in the back, a nasty glance from a man in a suit, but today, he noticed, nobody seemed to be going eastbound. The platform he was on was totally deserted, and the train, when it arrived, was empty. He sat down on the grubby, emerald-green seats. This lad was going to be a *cracking* wee player. By the time he'd got off the train, Euan was practically beside himself. He'd be the first, maybe even the *only* supporter there. Bodnar would remember him, that was for sure. In nine, ten, eleven years time, after his testimonial game at a tearful Parkhead, Lazlo would address the crowd in his halting, still heavily-accented English – "Ven feerst aye came to Glassgo, nabaddy know who Lazlo Bodnar vas… Nabaddy eckcep vun yunk man…"

Euan was snatched abruptly from his daydream by the need to urinate. In the phosphorescent light of the

Subway, a red sign pulsed meaningfully at the bottom of some stairs. *TOILETS*. Gratefully, Euan clattered down the cream-coloured steps and into the gents.

As he stood in front of the wide metal trough, relieved, he closed his eyes and allowed himself his dream. Overhead, the dreadful undulations of the train turned into a Parkhead roar.

"Ven feerst aye came to Celtic...."

Chih-CHOOM, chih-CHOOM...

"Nabaddy know who I am...

Chih-CHOOM, chih-CHOOM...

"Aye am alonn wiffout a fwent in der werld!"

Chih-CHOOM, chih-CHOOM...

"Eckcept...."

Chih-CHOOM...

"Except..."

CHOOM!!!!

The whole room shook, seemed to tilt crazily to one side. Water sloshed out of the urinal in a single gigantic wave, like the blade of a knife, sending yellow cubes of disinfectant everywhere. The lights, without warning, snapped off.

"Fuck…"

Euan stood still in the dark, breathing heavily. He could hear nothing and see nothing. Sensationless, it was just as he might have imagined Death, but for the wet patches on his jeans that clung to his thighs. He wondered what had happened. Had someone thrown themselves onto the tracks? But there was no screaming. No shouting. Nothing. Just the eerie dribble of water trickling back into the trough.

Eventually, his eyes started to get accustomed to the dark. The familiar shapes of a few minutes ago loomed vividly out of the black, like a photo negative of the original room. He stumbled, splashing, towards the door.

When he got out into the sunlight, he realised with a start that he was blinder than he had been in the darkness. The light slashed at him, filled his pupils with an assortment of neons and ochre blues. Shielding his eyes with his forearm he stared down at the comforting black of his shadow as it crept along the pavement. From everywhere the brightness blinded him, bouncing off windows and whitewashed walls. It was like that time at school, he thought, when the sun had washed the snowdrifts an agonising white. There was a strangely chemical smell in the air, he noticed, not unlike chlorine. He assumed it was the toilet disinfectant that had saturated his clothes.

His eyes adjusted, and he looked up. The street was empty. Trudging on past the River Clyde, through Glasgow Green, up Bridgeton way, he saw not another living soul. Not on foot, not by car – nothing. Was everyone away to these daft meetings like his mum, protests or whatever they were? A terrible thought, unbidden, entered his mind. Maybe Bodnar *was* a load of rubbish. His hands shook in his pockets as he contemplated it. Yes, that was it. He was rubbish. Six months time, three substitute appearances later, and it's back to Ferencvaros on loan, never to be seen again. Euan steadied himself, stuck the dangling ends of his scarf back into his hoodie. Turning onto London Road, Celtic Park loomed suddenly on the horizon. No, no sense in turning back now, he thought. Might as well go through with it.

Still, though. *Nobody?* Euan glanced over his shoulder, as if expecting the entire population of Glasgow to jump back out with a snigger. All the times he had been turned away by parents at front doors, briskly informed that so-and-so wasn't home, then looked up just in time to see the face at the window, the bedroom curtain twitching back again. If the whole city had chosen to play that game with him, he would not have been surprised. But when he looked back along the street, the only signs of life had been the faint splotches of his own footprints, rapidly drying on the concrete warmth.

As he approached it in the pale light of the afternoon, the stadium looked squat and alien. Girders curled like claws above its stands, as if the ground was a robotic hand bursting from a pile of rubble. As Euan drew closer, he realised that there were no cars, no people - no security guards, even. The great, smoked-glass doors to the stadium lay gapingly open. Euan searched for a sign – a cordon, a clipboard, an inviting arrow on a metal pole – but there was nothing. He crept up to the entrance and stood for a moment, peering into the gloom. A reception desk, unmanned. A cartful of drinks, untouched. On the floor, the crest of Celtic F.C., woven neatly into the carpet. He stood on his tip-toes and strained his neck this way and that, struggling to peer around distant, silent corners.

Nothing. So he went in.

***

Euan had been on stadium tours before, a rigorous frogmarch of bored mums and polite foreigners; but now, as the evidence of interrupted life piled up around him – letters left half-opened, jackets hung on hooks – he began to realise that something had gone terribly wrong, here, maybe everywhere. He remembered, vaguely, the headlines he'd seen on the front of newspapers as he'd skipped to the back, strange clusters of verbless nouns – TALKS, TENSIONS, MISSILES, FALLOUT. What had happened, he wondered? Had everyone been evacuated? And if so, why hadn't he? He had the sudden, awful feeling that he had done something wrong by not being rescued. Movie visions swallowed him, military men with barrels blazing, civilians who'd seen something they'd never been meant to, quarantines from which no living thing emerged. He peered out of an office window at the lifeless sky. He would not go back out there if he could help it.

Besides, there was surely plenty enough of everything in here to get by. He harvested all the keys he could find, rooting through handbags and office drawers as he gradually worked his way up through the corridors. He had always been fascinated by the implied exclusivity of keys. A key represented a place you could go where no one else could get you. But as his pockets started to fill up with them, sharp little clumps that bit his hands and scratched his legs through the holes, their dull weight suddenly became intolerable to him, and he emptied them out, strewing them on the carpet like the pieces of a jigsaw. He soon discovered that the only locked doors in the building were those of the executive suites, and those he had open in the matter of a moment, the double doors swinging aside to reveal a salon of ungodly cleanliness, a plush, pristine newness sharper than the pages of a freshly-printed book. He stared helplessly. A minibar on one wall, piled high with snacks. A TV in the corner, telephone by the door. Magnificent recliners stretched out in the half-dim alongside a wall-length window, covered by blinds of white and green. He had never seen anything like it.

Trembling, he reached out for a dangling loop of string and started to pull. Slowly, silently, the blinds began to rise. Light spilled into the room as if arriving from a different universe. As the blinds went up and up, details filled themselves in. The seats, green and white, crammed together in tight rows like corn on a cob. The pitch, luscious, mouth-watering, greener than nature. On the far side the stairs, yellow, climbing towards the descending sun as it slunk beneath the roof. And in seats, in white, the single word spelled out: CELTIC.

**

For Euan, the first few days at Celtic Park proved to be a reasonably cheerful proposition. After hours of searching fruitlessly for a back-up generator – a search he had reluctantly abandoned when he realised that he'd no idea what a back-up generator looked like, or how to work one – Euan had more or less accustomed himself to life without electricity. The mobile phones that lay around, the laptops on the desks – these still worked, but with no network to connect to and no power to recharge them, they were virtually useless. Whiling away an hour or two playing *Snake* or *Solitaire*, Euan wondered occasionally if the Internet still existed. He didn't know how to imagine that it didn't.

The electricity was off and the phone lines were down, but the water was still running, although what this meant about life outside Glasgow Euan couldn't tell. Not that he used the water, anyway; it was too cold to bathe in, and there was plenty of bottled stuff to drink. Food was not much more of a concern. The fridges in the kitchen had failed, leaving very little salvageable, and the crisps and nuts in the minibars would only stretch so far. But there'd been a decent little stash of sustenance in the physio's room – sports supplements, vitamins, energy drinks – and he'd managed to get by.

The first couple of weeks at Celtic Park passed quite quickly. The range of merchandise in the club's MegaStore had occupied him for hours on end; before long, everything he used, wore or ate bore the Celtic badge. At night he read player autobiographies by torchlight, huddling under blankets marked *Baby Bhoy*, his hand deep in a bowl of green and white Skittles. By day he was out on the pitch making stories of his own, an ongoing epic of cup final winners and derby-day deciders, racing to the Celtic End with the ball in the net and one hand up to the sky. That was where he was now, practicing his free-kicks from twenty yards out. His latest effort had just been blasted high into the seats and was ricocheting noisily around the stand. Nose wrinkled in disgust, he stared down at his brand-new boots, and at the threadbare turf around   them.

Truth was, by now he was starting to worry. Parkhead had been a lucky find, there was no doubt about that – its gigantic emptiness had sheltered him, somehow, from the gigantic emptiness outside. He still had no idea what was going on out there, if anything. That there were other living things around was clear, but he knew this more by inference than experience – the birdshit on the statues outside, for instance. And that was another thing, how quickly everything fell apart with no-one there to maintain it. He had tried manfully to keep the stadium in perfect condition; cleaning the floor, polishing the trophies, locking everything up at night. But it had got too much for him, and things had started to slide. First it was the statues. Then the manager's office, now a filthy storeroom of balled-up socks and shirts. Finally, even the trophy cabinets ceased to inspire his reverential awe. In fact, the shirt he was wearing now was the same one Stevie Chalmers had worn in the 1967 European Cup final. The mannequin it had previously adorned in a glass cabinet in the museum now wore instead an inside-out away shirt Euan had scored his first Parkhead 'goal' in. He had regretted the swap almost instantly, but it was too late by then. Room by room, Celtic Park was becoming a smaller and smaller place.

He headed back up the tunnel and got changed. He'd kept track of the days by a fixture calendar on the changing room wall. It was the end of July, now – Celtic's first game would have been a week today, at home to the Accies. Easy win. On the same day, Rangers were due to play Hearts. The Rank Gers versus the Purple Hun, he thought. There's a game to turn the stomach.

He found himself wondering what Ibrox was like now. He had seen it from the outside – it was visible from his old bedroom – but he'd never been in. Would he ever get a better chance? Not that he was planning to stay there or anything, he assured himself, he'd just be going over to check on his old house, see if there were any signs of life. What harm could it do to take a wee peek at Castle Greyskull as well?

He went out into the car-park. There were no cars in it, but the bicycle racks were full. He wheeled the first bicycle out of the shelter and onto the road. It was a clear day, bluish-tinged and silent. Swinging himself up onto the saddle, and with a few exploratory jabs at the pedals, Euan wobbled off down Kinloch Street and onto London Road.

***

61

It had been a long time since Euan had ridden a bike. He trembled minutely from one side to the other in balance, like a tossed coin settling on a table. Eventually he got into his stride, and it was not long before he was hurtling wildly through the empty streets. Nothing, as far as he could tell, had changed – even the cone on the Wellington Statue's head was still there. As he blasted through the inert traffic lights, his heart raced at the prospect of extending his dominions. Was Glasgow, after all this, his? He felt himself the awe of the living buildings, the wonder of the world. As he reached the Hielanman's Umbrella, an old railway bridge in the city's centre, he instinctively ducked; too large, he thought, to pass beneath untroubled.

The family home was just as he'd left it. For a moment at the driveway's foot he paused, convinced himself of signs of visitation; a mangled curtain, the garden gate ajar. The grass had grown, long and thick and seasoned, sprinkled with yellow dots of dandelion heads. But that was all. He cycled off down Copland Road, past the Subway station, and onto Edmiston Drive.

It was a dismal part of town. As he dismounted from his bike and wheeled it up to the big blue gates, Euan felt a pleasurable twinge of contempt at the ugliness of Ibrox Stadium, that grim little redbrick shoebox with the feel of an old swimming baths. On the walls, the residual flecks of long-removed graffiti, a scrap from a torn-down poster. Laying his bike to rest against the fence, Euan had a sense of dead religion, of sepulchres and Sunday Schools, tuneless church pianos hidden by musty curtains.

Suddenly, and without warning, an arm was wrapped around his neck, his chin locked tight in the crook of someone's elbow. Instinctively his hands flew up, clawing for space against the naked forearm. A knee thudded awkwardly into his buttock, and at the side of his neck pressed something hard, and metal, and sharp. Then it had a voice, whatever it was, a voice so close he could feel its saliva burst against his ear.

"What d'ye call a Billy with a knife?" it hissed. Euan struggled in its grasp for a moment, fighting for the breath to answer.

"A Tim opener."

The arm uncoiled abruptly from his neck and pushed him violently away. He staggered forward a few steps, wheezing and choking, his eyes full of water.

"That's right," his attacker said. He looked like he was a couple of years older than Euan, but so did everyone. His face scowled out from between a beanie and a puffy jacket, both blue; in his hand was a Stanley knife, big and black, with a wicked triangle of blade poking out. It looked heavy, dangling in the boy's grasp like it was hung from a tree with string.

"Might've known," he spat, looking Euan up and down, "The only ones left, eh – cockroaches and Celtic supporters."

Euan, still gasping, raised himself up, and looked steadily back.

"Aye, I was about to say much the same thing myself." The boy's face did not flicker one bit. The corner of blade on his knife retracted abruptly into the handle, which he stuffed into his pocket.

"A Fenian with a sense of humour. It must be the end of the world, right enough. C'mon in, I'll give you the guided tour." He rattled a fire exit with the sole of his boot, and it lurched obligingly open on its broken hinges. As the other lad held open the door, Euan hesitated on the threshold, staring in at the dingy white corridor.

"It's alright," the boy tersely assured him, "You'll no set on fire or anything. You're invited in. So on ye go."

Euan glanced longingly at his bike, then at the boy. He felt in his pockets for any sort of a weapon, but his keys were all he had. Reluctantly, and with one last look at the sky, he stepped through into the dark, the heavy clang of the door behind him rattling his bones.

***

On the inside, Ibrox was much the same as it had looked from the road. Everything within was dirt and dust, old paint and old carpets. As they wandered round, his companion - whose name he had now gathered was Gary - kept up a running commentary on everything they were looking at, a soliloquy which combined the hyperbolic language of the tour guide with the droning delivery of the punter.

"With its traditional period features an its Victorian grandness," Gary monotoned, his face entirely blank, "Ibrox provides a sombre an dignified ambiance entirely in keeping with…"

"Aye, aye," Euan cut in, "That's good, that, but how's aboot tellin us how *you* got here?"

Gary paused for thought.

"I walked," he said, finally. Euan couldn't tell if he was joking.

"I don't mean that, I mean where *is* everybody?" Gary shook his head slowly.

"I don't know. Deid or that. I'm no bothered."

He lumbered on. Euan stared after him for a second, silently.

"How'd ye mean?" he demanded, "Are ye serious? Are they really *deid*?"

"If they're no, they might as well be, for all the good they're doing *me*," Gary answered, shrugging his shoulders, "Anyways. The Argyle House Restaurant is a favourite destination for celebrations an special occasions…"

As they plodded around on Gary's guided tour, Euan continued to press him for information. *What had happened? How had he got here? Did he know about any others?* But it became dismally apparent to him that the lad was no more clued up than he was. Gary had no conception at all of the amount of time that had passed, or the order things had happened in; listening to him just made Euan question his own chronologies. As he gazed around the function suite they were in, his eyes alighted on a green rectangle stretched out on a table.

"Here!" he pointed, "Whit's that?" Gary's eulogy of the club's partnership scheme ground to a halt, and he wheeled slowly round to face the table.

"Och, that's Subbuteo," he answered, "I found it in the Megastore. It's a table fitba game…"

"I *know* whit Subbuteo is," Euan said, getting closer, "I used to have one when I was wee. I didn't know they made it anymore."

"They don't. They're deid."

"I mean *before* that," Euan snapped, "Christ Almighty! No wonder you lot are nearly extinct."

Euan strolled around the table in wonder. It was brand new. The green fabric, covered in pitch linings so fresh they were almost sticky. The little players on their semi-spherical bases. A shiny plastic trophy, nearly as big as the goals, lay in its own plastic alcove in the box. With his fingernail he flicked the ball; its roll was perfect and true. It was his bedroom now, his house, back before all this had happened.

"Are ye wanting a game…?" Gary asked, haltingly.

"Bagsy Celtic," Euan answered immediately.

"Bagsy Rangers!" Gary said, almost simultaneously.

"For the cup?" Euan said, prizing it out of the box.

"You're on."

As he bent over the table arranging his players, Euan looked up for a moment to find Gary standing there motionless, his hand extended out across the pitch. His grimy palm looked painfully exposed, caught between the brand-new blue of his jacket and the clean green of the felt. Lifting his own hand to meet it, Euan found himself leaning imperceptibly backwards, as if the entire floor were at a subtle tilt. As their hands meshed over the centre circle, he was surprised for a moment by how hard and warm it was. He had forgotten what other people felt like.

***

"My dad always used tae say I kicked the arse out of everything," Euan said, thoughtfully. Gary glanced up from his players.

"My dad never."

They were sitting in the centre circle at Ibrox, the Subbuteo pitch stretched out between them. It was half-time and conditions were perfect. Euan stared up into the sky, hugging his knees to his chest.

"Whit a day."

Gary squinted upwards.

"Aye." He cleared his throat awkwardly, and assumed the nasal twang of a tannoy announcement. "Substitution for Rangers. Comin off, number 8, Joao Silverio. Replacin him, number 17, Robert MacTaggart!" Euan raised his eyebrow quizzically.

"When did he come back?" Gary shrugged.

"He's came out of retirement for the big game, eh? Championship decider and that."

"That's a sentiment selection, that. MacTaggart's a spent force. I only hope yer chairman shares yer lofty ideals."

From that first game all those weeks ago the idea had quickly swollen, first to a second match, then to a league, and eventually to a whole season, with cup competitions, reserve matches, friendlies and testimonials. Home and away they played, each day one cycling over to the other with their team underarm   and their latest news.

"MacDonald's injured," Gary would report breathlessly, chaining up his bike, "Our only other keeper's cup-tied. We're havin to play Wallace in goal."

"You think you've got problems?" Euan responded scornfully, "Martinez has just went walkaboot. Nobody kens *where* he is. Says he's no comin' back 'til he gets a new contract."

"Promises, promises, eh? Ach well, show us doon tae the changin room then, I've got a few things I need tae go over."

From their respective trophy rooms they had dug out a bewildering array of vases, cups, shields and plates, which changed hands on a weekly basis. Men of the match were recognised and rewarded, post-match interviews were held – after a particularly comprehensive victory Gary had even staged an open-top bus tour.

"YA DANCEEEEEEEERRRRRR!" he'd howled, pelting up London Road on his bike with a tin cup held above his head. "CHAMPIONIEEES!"

"Aye, good work, the B&Q Cup, eh, quality," Euan observed moodily on the pavement, "Ma pal's uncle won that as well, so well done there."

Emboldened by each other's company, they had started to cast their net beyond the immediate horizons of Ibrox and Celtic Park. Sometimes they played football on the streets, sprawling games of Nutmeg and Cuppie which took them from one end of Argyle Street clean to the other. But everything else, they realised now, had run on electricity; and without it the cinemas and the department stores were dark and silent warehouses.

They'd ridden to Hampden Park once, where Scotland used to play, with a view to staging a cup final. It was locked up tight, no chance of getting in, but it had got them thinking.

"D'ye ever wonder aboot expandin the league?" Gary had asked as they sat on the Hampden stairs.

"Eh?"

"I mean, d'ye think there's other folk in other stadiums?" Gary went on, "Like Partick Thistle an that?"

"Ah dunno, Gary," Euan said, "D'ye no think we'd know aboot it by noo?"

"Aye, maybe," the big fella had granted, "But likesay doon south? Folk always used to say Rangers an Celtic should go doon south."

"Ach, I'm happy enough here, Gary."

"Aye, me too. Me too."

Today was the last day of the league, and it was neck and neck. Gary was really going for it, throwing caution to the winds, but Euan had perfected a strategy of ball-retention which left him chasing shadows.

"Playin the Celtic way, is it?" Gary grunted, "That's a joke. Same old, same old, an ye call it a tradition."

Euan smiled and said nothing. Time was running out. Desperately, Gary advanced his entire team in one long row, like a chessboard of pawns. Euan, flustered, misplaced a pass. The stop-watch clicked, beeped, and stopped.

"Here, that's time…"

He didn't get to finish. Gary had already smashed the ball into the net so hard that a handful of players had been carried in there with it. The whole pitch was pandemonium, figures rolling hither and thither on their sides like pins on a bowling alley. Euan stared down at them in wordless dismay.

"You cheating Orange *bastard*..." he spluttered, incredulously.

"How that?" Gary retorted. "There was injury time!"

"There weren't *any* injuries," Euan spat back, furiously, "But it wasn't for want of tryin, I'll grant you."

"Whit ye tryin to say?" Gary rose to his feet ominously. Euan picked himself up too, sweeping his players up in brisk handfuls. His entire body was shaking.

"You know whit I'm sayin," he said, refusing to look up, "Once a Hun, always a Hun, once a cheat, always a cheat."

"How…"

"Folk like you," he was so angry now he was almost crying, "I know folk like you! You're quick enough with your knives, eh? You're handy enough with your fists! Aye. It's folk like you that give the rest of us a bad name. 'They're all as bad as each other'. Naw. It's *youse*. Youse are the ones."

Gary had fallen silent now. His arms hung limply by his sides. Euan shook his head in contempt.

"I'm away. I'm no bothered if I never see this dump again. They Koreans, or whoever it was – they had the right idea."

As he stormed off up the tunnel, Euan remembered that he had left the league trophy out on the pitch. He went to go back, but the sight of Gary hunched over, picking up his players one by one, stopped him dead. Turning, he tore his teamsheet off the changing room door and ran off up the stairs. He had not cried for anything yet, and was not about to start now. He made it all the way to the fire exit before bursting into tears.

***

The next morning, Gary did not come. Nor the next, nor the next. As one day drifted into another, Euan, who had stopped marking time on the calendar, lost count. He pretended it was the close-season, and spent hours at a time in the manager's office, preparing. At nights on his recliner, struggling to sleep, he'd stare out the window at the ghostly pitch, listening to the creak of girders in the wind. He could hardly believe that this stadium, this club, with its hundred years of history and thousands of supporters, all that was left of it was him, and his plastic players, and his daydreams. It terrified him.

Weeks passed. Months, he supposed. He plucked up the courage to ride ever closer to Ibrox; Glasgow Green, Argyle Street, nearly into Govan, once. Finally, one cold night, after visiting his house, he closed his eyes and forced himself to cycle all the way there. He had no clear idea what he was going to do or say; but when he arrived, he found the place quiet and empty. The league trophy was still out where he had left it, half-full of rain. The Subbuteo pitch was gone.

Back at Celtic Park again, the solitude engulfed him. He had never been lonely before – he had never had friends. Every day he rode back and forth to Ibrox, just in case. Some nights he even slept there, getting up in the middle of the night to count the bicycles, read the stadium guide. Check the doors weren't locked. It was darker there now than ever before, but he had come to know its corridors well, those walls of ceramic tiles and ornate wood, like a cross between a church and a swimming baths. Sometimes it was so black that he couldn't tell if his eyes were open or not, and it reminded him how he used to scare himself as a child, shutting his eyes for so long that he forgot what colour looked like.

But it was the silence that scared him most of all, the sheer and awful scale of it; how it filled the stands at Celtic Park and towered steeply all around him in sky-high walls. To be alone upon the noiseless earth, and hear no stirring but the turmoil of your own breath; to find companionship in the plashing of the rain and the groaning of the lampposts in the wind; these were horrors of a particular kind he had never been prepared for.

His thoughts now, when they came, were cruel and dreadful visitors, and he took refuge from them wherever he could. He had long since exhausted the battery of every laptop he had, watching films and listening to music. Over at Ibrox he dug out a laptop so old that it didn't even have a CD drive. The hard drive was full of Rangers songs, the kind he'd used to hear outside his house. They had been threatening, then, flat, aggressive monotones sung by skinheads with red-rimmed eyes and expressionless faces. But now those men were gone, and nothing they had lived for mattered. When the screen on the laptop blinked and went abruptly blank, Euan sat there for a moment, listening to the last, tinny note of those voices as they faded quietly away. He didn't quite know why, but he felt like he somehow owed it to them to remember.

He left Ibrox and got back on his bike. The date on the laptop had been the May 26th. It was a Saturday, Cup Final day, according to the fixture list. He thought about riding up to Hampden Park, where the final would have been played. It seemed like the right thing to do. He set off down Edmiston Drive, noticing with fresh curiosity the landmarks along the way; the churches, the mosques, the public libraries. Things were not away to rack and ruin just yet, although the gutters were thick with leaves, and grass was bursting through the concrete cracks. He wondered what it was like at the Botanic Gardens now, whether the trees were swarming the fences yet, crashing upwards through the domes.

He had learned, over time, not to spend too much time inside. It was so dark indoors, and it only wound up making him miss the way that things had used to be. He stayed at Parkhead now because it was open to the sky, both indoors and outdoors at the same time. It could still be scary there in the dark, when the wind was howling in the tunnels and strange things were rustling across the pitch. On nights like those he found himself looking at the moon, wishing he was up there, just so he could get a better view of whatever it was that had happened.

And inside, you could forget what silence sounded like. In the stadiums, every noise was like a bomb going off, even if it was just a book falling off a table, his heartbeat. Out here, on the narrow roads to Hampden, there was still noise – the jingling of his backpack, the sticky burr of pedals going round – but it was all soaked up into the silence, like water into a scrap of paper, as if noise just made the quiet *louder*. Something smelled like damp, but he couldn't remember it having rained. In fact, it seemed like there had been no weather at all for a long time; no rain, no snow, no anything. It was as if someone who was leaving had switched off the sky.

Hampden rose above the city on gigantic staircases, like a spider waking from sleep. Euan hadn't thought about how he was going to get in, or what he was going to do there, but he would work it out. He had keys in his pocket, and there was so much of Glasgow that he had never seen; he would have to take better care of it than he had of Celtic Park. He dumped his bike untidily at the foot of the stairs, and began his long ascent to the top, where the fire escape was singing inaudibly on its broken hinge. Then the wind was racing him, and the leaves flew past like emissaries. The forest was on its way.

The Eye of the Needle

In summer the Keenans always stayed indoors. On winter's nights you might glimpse one of them, standing forgotten at the bottom of the road, a short, stiff duffel coat tapering to a gnome-like head; but they burned easily. Their skin was soft as sallow clay and coloured like sawdust, as if Time itself had already started to rasp away at them. Their house overlooked a threadbare scrub where football was played, and bored goalkeepers often watched their curtainless windows for hours; sometimes a pallid, moon-like face would arise in the upstairs glass and stare, but usually the only sign of life was the waning blue of a broken TV. Never in their lives had the Keenans been known to buy something - everything they owned had been hauled from a skip or gifted by a neighbour - and the back garden of their semi-detached was a necropolis of suburban dreams, a ruinous clutter of broken toys and furniture. Even on a sunny afternoon, the two boys threaded their way through the mess with care - everybody knew somebody who had found a needle there.

"Ah *hate* this," Stuart wailed miserably, lifting his little legs high into the air, "Can we no just go the long way roond, Ally? Can we no just…"

"Shut *up*." His big brother snapped without looking at him. "We're late enough as it is. It's yer own stupid fault anyway, wearin sandals tae play fitba in. Ah *telt* ye we were cuttin through the Keenans's."

"Aye but…"

"Aye *nothin*," Ally kicked a ball with a dent in its side and sent it skittering across the dirt. "It's bad enough needin tae… Hullo!"

So homogenous was the muddle that they hadn't noticed the smallest Keenan until they'd almost fallen over him, propped up against a pile of foul-smelling carpet. From the depths of a duffle coat shiny with wear, little hands peeped out to clutch a roller skate. His listless fingers birred a single wheel, the ragged yellow plastic rattling on the axle.

"Och, it's just wee Waw-waw." Ally said. "Ye daein awright there, pal?"

Waw-waw looked up at them wordlessly, his face contorted in a permanent squint as if the entire world were made of light. His real name was William, but 'Waw-waw' was the most he'd ever been heard to make of it. It was the only thing, in fact, they'd ever heard him say.

"Comin for a game, Waw-waw? Show us some of your skills?" Ally asked, not unkindly. Waw-waw shook his head very seriously and went back to spinning his wheel.

"Moan, Ally," Stuart hissed, hopping nervously on the spot. He had heard the same stories as everybody else about the Keenans, and was still young enough to believe them.

"Aye, in a minute," Ally said, intrigued suddenly by the remains of an old rocking horse. The hollow plastic had been worn clean of all the colour that once identified it as a horse, and the rusty mechanism screeched rhythmically as it swayed. He tilted his head, listening, then placed his eye to a small round hole where the saddle once had been.

"Here!" he exclaimed. "There's money in there!"

"Ally, *moan*," Stuart whimpered again.

"Aye but, listen!" Ally gave the horse another shove. It rang with the tell-tale jingle of coins.

"Waw-waw!" he shouted, "Listen! There's money in this rockin horse! Ah'll go ye halfers when ah get back, eh!"

Waw-waw glanced up blankly at them. Dark green wellingtons with radiator scars ran all the way up to his knees. Stuart shook his head.

"Just leave him, Ally. He disnae even know whit money *is*."

Ally didn't say anything, but gave the horse another demonstrative shove.

"Buried treasure!" he enunciated slowly, "Pieces of eight! Doubloons, Waw-waw! You leave it tae me, pal. Ah'll sort it oot."

The squint on Waw-waw's face left no room for anything else. His eyes were horizontal gashes in his yellow skin, like lines drawn in putty with the point of a knife. He looked back down without saying anything. For a moment, the only sound in the garden was the expiring whirr of the skate's wheel. Ally cleared his throat.

"Awright, Waw-waw, that's settled then. Partners, eh? Listen, ah've got somethin else on the noo, but ah'll catch ye later, right?"

He backed off towards the gate, where Stuart was still waiting for him. They stopped for a moment and watched as Waw-waw, completely oblivious, placed his hand inside the skate and rolled it on the grass.

"Boy's no got a Scooby," Ally said, quietly, "Must be aboot three or four quid in there. Ach well, it's his money tae. Fair's fair an that, ye know."

Stuart nodded, relieved. With a last backward glance at the horse and the garden, he pulled shut the wooden gate.

"Right enough, Ally. Fair's fair."

With the boys gone, silence crept back into the garden like a startled pet. Waw-waw was glad. He hadn't liked the bigger boy, or his friend, or the fuss they'd made. It had frightened him a little. His parents got that way too, about money, tiny little bits of it. Sometimes they found some, down the back of the couch or in someone else's pockets. Then things got worse.

Waw-waw got to his feet. The horse was still rocking a little. He laid his grubby hand upon it, waiting for it to stop. He had remembered something. From his pocket he pulled out an old two pence, almost green with age, and pushed it into the hole in the top of the rocking horse. It was too big to fit, but he hammered it with his fist until it went through, falling into the pile with a small and hollow jingle.

He rocked the horse carefully with his palm. It sounded like an awful lot of money. For a moment there he listened to the lulling rhythm of the coins, scraping around in the horse's belly where they could do no harm to anyone. To do even that much had taken him a long time. Idly, he wondered how much more money there was left, and if it would all fit inside his horse. He hoped it would. It was a big horse, and even pounds were really only very small.

Auld Airchie's Losin It

Haudin ma hauns up, boays. Me, ah never even noticed it. Hing is, tae, we'd hid a wee bash fur im uppit the clubhoose the week afore an he wis *fine*. Honest tae God, ye wid never o guessed! Eighty-two year auld 'n' loupin aboot like a billy goat. Even goat im up gien it wan o they auld Harry Lauder songs. Tell ye whit, fur an auld fella he's no half goat a voice oan im. Usetae be wan o the best wee crooners in the Nitsie, folk wis tellin us. Fair took them back tae the auld days. Then he goes takes a heider doon the stairs an everybody's laughin an sayin, well, that takes them back tae the auld days tae.

Ah mean he wis fine an that, eh, nae herm done, but it's past wan an his eyes is gaun thigither, so we we goat him in a taxi an sent him up the road. Auld fella can hardly walk his length bi then, so ah says ah'd go wae him, ye know, wait 'n' return, like. Well, when we git there auld Margaret's still up waitin fur him.

"Ye daft auld scunner!" she says when he shuffles in, "You get tae yer bed! Don't bother gaun *near* that kitchen!"

Bi the time she goat him in a cup o tea he'd fell asleep in the chair, bent double like, so's the tip o his bunnet's touchin his knee. Folk at the club wis fawin ower themselves when ah telt them. Next time we sees im he's goat a black eye an two plasters oan his heid, like he's Oor bloody Wullie or suhin.

"Aw that oan a wee boattle o Grouse!" Everybody's killin themsels laughin. "Och, yir some man, so ye ur!"

Bit we didnae hink anythin else o it. Ah mean, that wis jist Airchie.

***

Anywey, next hing is we're aw up the clubhoose an Mary McKinnon's sittin there wae her rum an coke, no sayin anythin. Well, we're aw hinkin she's jist in a cream puff aboot suhin, mebbe goat a new haircut 'n' naebody's said anyhin, when she jist came right oot wae it.

"Here!" she says, bangin her gless oan the table, "D'ye no think auld Airchie's losin it?"

"Eh?" We aw turn tae look. Couple o tables ower they're passin a wallet roon wi a photae o somebody's wean. Everybody's smilin an noddin away, an Airchie's staunin there an aw, watchin them ower the tap o his sunglesses. Then somedy hauns im the wallet an they're aw gushin aboot this wean an clappin im oan the shooder.

"D'ye no think auld Airchie's losin it?" Mary says in that wey, ye ken. She took a sip o her straw, but there wis nuhin left so it jist made the ice-cubes rattle. "*Ah* hink he's definitely losin it."

Well, auld Mary's a blether, right enough, but then when ye looks at it, like, it starts tae add up. Ah mean, ye'll hiv noticed it yersel, the wey he jist stauns there when ye're talkin tae him, no sayin anyhin, jist *listenin* tae ye. Then when he says suhin it's dead quiet like, so's ye can hardly hear it, an it's nuhin tae dae wi whit ye were talkin aboot. An the wey he walks aboot! Shouldae seen im gittin up they stairs when we were watchin the ammies. It wis like wan o they mummies fae a horror film. Ah mean, ah ken he's knockin oan a bit, but that's no right, that. That's no normal. So we're aw talkin aboot it, an everybody's pittin in their ain wee tuppenceworth, an that's when we realise it's true – the poor fella's oan is wey oot. Auld Airchie's losin it.

Took a wee while fur word tae git roon. It's no like Mary's wan fur keepin secrets, but when that stuff aboot Betty Hislop's man came oot, Airchie kindae goat pit oan the back burner. Still, wance that wis sortit oot, the auld fella wis right back oan the agenda. Ah mean, it wis

Margaret ah felt sorry fur. We aw did. The auld yin, like, he disnae hiv a Scooby, hinks it's aw business as usual. Likesay, *we're* aw noticin it – forgettin his doakter's appointment, turnin up at a funeral wae a button oaf his shirt – but he's happy as Larry, eh, no bothered. An naebdy's wantin tae say anythin tae Margaret cause that's the last hing she's needin, in't it, some hackit auld beesom tellin er her man's the talk o the steamie. Bit ye kin *tell*, like, it's gittin ower much fur er. Did ye see her up the jumble sale, at the chapel hall? Honest tae God. There's her auld fella gaun jist aboot doolally, hardly rememberin tae wash is face in the moarnin, an she's oot foldin claes an makin tea! The poor auld sowel, ah don't know how she copes. God knows, he wis hard enough work even when he wisnae gaun aff is heid.

Aye, so, we aw goat thigither up the club, eh, see aboot arrangin suhin fur the auld lad afore he's too faur gone tae appreciate it. A testimonial or a presentation night or that. Mebbe even name a trophy efter im. "The Archie MacPherson Memorial Cup". Nice ring tae it, eh? It'd jist be cawed the Archie MacPherson Cup tae begin wi, bit we'd git the engraver tae leave a space. Save buyin a new yin later, ye know. Jist tryin tae be practical.

Cause it's nae picnic, like. Ah mean, it's no easy. It's a terrible hing tae say, but ye git right fed-up listenin tae im say the same hings aboot his grandweans, or his great-grandweans or whatever it is, ower an ower again. The young yins, the players, they're guid wi him. Take the piss a wee bit sometimes, eh, but they're never done buyin him drinks an that. Gaun up when he's at the bar, yappin Trish's ear aff. "Whit you chitterin aboot noo, eh, auld yin? Haw Trish, another Scotch fur ma wee pal Airchie!" Thank Christ fur that. Gies the rest o us a minute tae ursells. That's aw ah'm sayin.

Still, we're needin tae git sumhin soartit oot. We've been meanin tae ask Mary whit she thought aboot this trophy idea. It's no like we kin ask Margaret, an Mary's jist goat a better kind o… ah don't know… a better kind o *sense* aboot the auld fella. Sometimes ye'll be lookin at him talkin tae somedy quite the thing, an ye'll hink tae yersel, well, mebbe there's nuhin *wrang* wi him, efter aw. Then Mary'll say "Aye, he's in good fettle the night, bless im, but it'll no last," an next hing ye know he's scrabblin aboot under the table fur a fifty pence he says he's droapped. She usetae work up the nursin home, Mary did. She kens whit she's oan aboot. So wur meanin tae ask her aboot it, this trophy ah mean, if she hinks it's a guid idea, but she's no been in aw week. Usually never away fae the place! Left her hoose keys here oan Saturday there, so ye'd hink she'd hiv been in bi noo.

Best o it is, tae, Airchie's been right chipper the last couple o days. Sin she's no been here tae see it. Worries hersel sick aboot the auld boay. Curtains in her hoose her drawn an aw. Mebbe she's goat hersel anither fella oan the go. Ye never ken wi yon Mary. She's a fly yin, her.

Johnny-on-the-Spot

Big Johnny Fotheringham was the best striker of a ball we'd ever had at the club, and the best liar too, which was saying a great deal. Most fellas wound up playing for Thistle, they had a history they needed forgotten – a fly bet on the side, a year's ban under a different name – but Johnny showed up at training one day clean as a whistle, far as we knew, with his Hi-Tec boots and an air of puzzled concentration. Deano had him claimed before the end of warm-up.

"Leave this yin tae me, ma wee disciples," Deano told us as we gathered round, Johnny still star-jumping his way across, "Ah'll take care o the introductions."

So that was Johnny getting the lolly knocked off his stick big-time, even before we knew his name. Only, it didn't happen. Soon as Johnny was shoe-horned into his training bib he fired in a volley, a cannonball of a shot, which set the whole goal to trembling like a cable in the wind.

"Good hit," Deano muttered, barely audible above the electric hum of the stanchions.

"Didnae quite get it right," Johnny responded, tramping down an invisible divot with his boot, "Postage-stamp top-corner, shouldae been."

Deano's mouth set into a line, his fingers curling suddenly at the end of his arms. But he didn't have time to move before the ball was in the goal again, spinning impossibly up the inverse slope of the net. Deano's gaze lingered on Johnny like a two-pence on a nearly-won scratchcard.

"Whit were ye aimin fur there, then?" he croaked. "The top corner at the Bernabau?"

"It's these baws," Johnny shook his head disdainfully, "They're too light. Wee tap an BANG! Back o the net."

"Ah suppose the baws are made ooty titanium where you come fae," Deano said, "The keepers as well."

But something happened as Deano turned away. His features converged in on his nose, like they'd been scrunched together by an invisible hand, and a long, simian arm curled over his head to scratch his opposite ear.

"Haw, skipper…" someone said.

"Shhh," Deano aimed a long finger at his own forehead, "Ah'm hivvin a wee Damascus moment here. The gears are turnin, boys, clickety-click. Haud oan."

He punted the ball as far out of play on Johnny's side as he could, then turned to the rest of us with a come-here gesture that managed to be a kind of violence. We crept over reluctantly, in pairs where possible. Deano clapped his hands together briskly.

"Right! Here's whit ah'm thinkin, laddies. Fair's fair. Youse melt *him* an ah'll melt *youse*. Get it?"

We did. When Johnny returned with the ball, it was to a very different game, one in which he bounded friskily through us like a muddy Labrador at a garden party. As we recoiled out of his way, he pulled the trigger on a shot which boomed hopelessly over the bar, squiggling in the air like an electron as it disappeared into the distance.

"Whit was that?" Deano asked in sudden, dismayed suspicion.

"The sun was in ma eyes," Johnny shrugged, squinting accusatively up at the overcast sky, "And these *boots*….!"

And for the rest of the day, whether we tackled him or no, Johnny continued to conjure up three parts divinity to

93

one part disaster, and all of them no sooner executed than excused, success dismissed as failure, and failure as freak. When training finally came to an end, with Johnny apologetically describing a thirty-yard piledriver as "a slice", Deano broke into his first jog of the day to catch up with the new boy before he got back to the changing rooms.

"So, where were ye playin before? Ah've never seen ye aboot."

"Oh, aye, here and there," Johnny mumbled, dusting the non-existent mud from his hands, "Doon south fur a bit. Professionally, ah mean. Ye widnae have heard o them."

"Try me," Deano said. "Ah used to play in England masel."

"Naw, no England, Australia, ah mean. Doon under."

"Zat right? Ma cousin's coachin in Melbourne, mebbe he'll have heard o ye?"

"Doubt it, ah never went near the place. It's awfy run-doon these days. Listen, ah'll need tae head, ah've a bus tae catch." Johnny began to accelerate away from us. Deano stared at him quizzically.

"Here, ah thought you drove here?" he shouted after him.

"Nah, ma car's at the garage," Johnny replied, picking up pace as Deano started to jog after him.

"But… But ah *saw* you gettin oot a motor this mornin when ye got here."

"Aye, but that was ma da giein us a lift. He cannae pick us back up cos he's goat work tae go tae." The casual nature of Johnny's stride did an admirable job of concealing the fact that, to all intents and purposes, he was now sprinting. Deano, who had the instincts of a terrier when it came to men in football boots running away from him, helplessly gave chase.

"Aye, but izzat no your motor there, though? Yon Fiesta?"

"Naw, it's just a really popular car," Johnny yelled over his shoulder, "Everybody's goat wan these days. That's me away, ah'll see ye on Tuesday!"

And with that he belted off around the wooden fence. We listened with wonder at the clitter-clatter of his studs as they slowed, halted, and then plodded reluctantly off to the bus stop.

***

It wasn't long before word got out, and men in club ties who we'd never seen before started turning up at the Thistle training ground, watching us through the windscreen of their Hondas or shivering by the sidelines in their coats. Each and every time, a few whispers from the gaffer would send Johnny dutifully over to shake hands and improvise apologies whilst Deano, the club captain, watched from the outskirts.

"Doon tae check the goods, ah see. *Here be dragons, boys,*" he'd said, pointing at the dividing white of the touchline, "Do not feed the animals."

After a few moments of vigorous nodding, Johnny would once again accept the limp, leathery claw offered him, and come back to us at a stiff trot.

"Hail the returnin hero!" Deano proclaimed with a curtsy, "Zat you away tae Bayern Munich then?"

"Naw, ah'm too busy the noo tae think ae gaun anywhere else," Johnny replied, scratching his chin in thought, "An ah'm needin my passport renewed first, anyroads."

"Oh aye," Deano said, "Izzat whit ye telt His Nibs over there?"

"Well, no exactly, ah…" Johnny's eyes darted from one invisible possibility to another before he blustered, "Ah mean, ah don't think it's right tae talk aboot other clubs till it's a done deal, ye know? It's no fair on youse lot."

Deano nodded and looked suitably touched.

"Ah appreciate that, Johnny, but c'mon." He laid his hand on Johnny's shoulder. "Look at it this wey. How much'd ye be worth? Ye're talkin ten, twenty million at least?"

"Ach, it's a crazy market," Johnny demurred, looking away bashfully, "Naebody's worth *that*."

"Right enough, pal," Deano enthused, "Couldnae agree mair. But that's the world we're livin in. So, let's say ten million for you. Have ye any idea whit the Thistle could do wi ten million pounds?"

Johnny digested this prospect uneasily, like a tenth cream doughnut of the day.

"Aye, but money isnae everythin," he finally murmured, "Plus ye'd have aw the agent's fees tae take aff that…" Deano cut him off with a wave of his hand.

"Ah know, ah know," he said, "An ye'd be lookin fur a wee wedge yersel, eh? Quite right tae, ye've goat tae look oot fur number wan. Plus ye'll be needin your passport renewed, an God knows that's an arm an a leg…"

"But ah don't need the money," Johnny's watery blue eyes were floundering desperately in his pallid face, "Ah'm daein' alright as it is… Ah don't want tae go tae Germany… An then ma granny's no been keepin weel lately…"

Just as it seemed like there would be no end, that Johnny would just keep stumbling on through his sentence like a drunk man crossing a dancefloor, a sharp whistle sent us off in all directions, retrieving balls, hauling nets, carrying cones. The man in the tie was gone by then, but if he had stuck around then even he might have noticed that Johnny was having a howler. For half an hour he plodded wearily around the midfield, like a man in a private nightmare, the game gradually winding to a worried halt around him.

Deano silenced us all with a gesture, took the ball, and laid it gently into Johnny's feet. Surprised, Johnny lashed it, without looking, into the bottom corner. There was a long, breathless hush. Birds chittered. Everyone stared at Johnny as he looked disapprovingly down at his spotless boots.

"Wrang fit," he croaked in disappointment, then turned and shuffled, back to the halfway line.

***

Nobody was surprised to see Johnny's name first on the Thistle teamsheet come the start of the season, and with him and Deano bossing things in midfield folk were talking about a big year ahead. Often as not in the early games Deano would come hobbling off with ten minutes left, having spent most of the ninety putting the boot on anyone who tried to get a whiff of Johnny. Two-nil up at Ayr with five minutes to go, he eased himself painfully down onto the bench beside me and started pulling the tape from his socks.

"Five goals in five games, eh. D'you think he can keep this up?" I asked.

"Aye, an five bookings in five games for *me*. Question is, can I?" Deano grunted. "Ninety minutes a game o stoppin anybody from touchin him in case he bursts oot greetin. Look at that."

He pulled off the tape to reveal a studmark the size of a bullet-hole in his right calf.

"That was meant for *him*. If this keeps up, ah'll be oot tae pasture before the year's done."

He leaned back for a moment against the porous concrete of the dugout, thinking.

"Still, though. If this is my last season… as long as I get a medal ooty it, that'll be fine by me."

Meanwhile, a murmur of confused disapprobation rolled around the stands as Johnny took a swing at a standing ball and missed. Deano shook his head wearily.

"Whit's up wi that, then? The easier ye make it for him, the harder he makes it fur himself. Have ye ever seen him score a penalty yet, even in trainin? Misses them every time. Ah… *AW REFEREEEE!!!*"

Deano, along with half the crowd, was up on his feet as Johnny took a header over a mistimed tackle. As he lay there on the turf with his hands around his calf, Deano turned a finger on the opposition dugout.

"*Cheats!* You're nothin but a bunch o hackin cheats!" He turned back to the bench, his voice dropping to a more contemplative volume. "Mind you, Johnny made a meal o that. If that's aw it takes tae pit him doon, we're finished soon as ah get ma first suspension…. Next week."

Deano's mouth tightened as Johnny limped off the pitch, one hand around the physio's shoulder, the other massaging his agonised face.

"Naw, naw. This'll no dae," Deano said, "It's no a flimmin crèche ah'm running here. This is gettin sorted."

And as the physio lowered Johnny gently onto the bench, Deano stood over them both, arms folded across his red-and-yellow chest.

"You alright Johnny?" he asked. "Were you doon lookin for your contact lens or somethin?"

"Ye kiddin?" Johnny grimaced, gingerly rolling his sock down. "He *nailed* me. Ah just managed tae git oot the way in time. If ah hidnae clocked him oot the corner o ma eye, he'd have had ma leg broken."

Deano put his hand over his mouth for a moment, rubbing his chin furiously as he stared out into the crowd.

"They reflexes o yours, eh?" he eventually piped up, much more breezily, "Ah hope Gerry Lennox got a note o that."

Johnny's head winched slowly up from his shoulders.

"Whit d'ye mean?" he asked.

101

"Gerry Lennox, the United scout?" Deano answered in surprise. "He's sittin over there… Aw, he's away noo. Must've left when you went aff. Ah thought you knew?"

Johnny dropped his head diffidently as he tangled with his muddy laces.

"Well, it's hard tae keep track. Ah leave that stuff tae ma agent…."

"Who's your…"

"But ah'm between agents the noo," Johnny continued hastily. "So that was auld Gerry finally made it, eh?

"Aye, must've been," Deano yawned, stretching his arms, "Mind, ah hope he left afore ye goat injured."

Johnny's head shot up from his boots much more quickly this time.

"Eh? How that?" he scowled.

"Well, ye know, big club like United, they're lookin fur the total package," Deano said airily, "They're investing a lot o time an' money in somebody, they're no wantin' a lad that's gonnae be crocked nine months oot the year."

"But…"

"Seen it happen a million times. Scout turns up tae a game. Boy gets sent aff?" Deano licked the end of an imaginary pencil and slashed a line in the air, "Name aff the list. Boy gits injured? Name aff the list. Noo, *ah* know you're no a malingerer – obviously, *ah* know that. But Gerry Lennox, aw he knows is that you came off in a big game wi five minutes left."

Johnny's eyes were suddenly overcast with gloom. His legs thrumming with nervous energy, he pulled himself up off the bench and stared forlornly out into the crowd.

"Ah widnae worry aboot it, son," Deano said, more gently this time, "Ah've a feelin he'll be back."

Johnny sighed and, with one last look, turned away.

"Disnae matter either way. There's plenty mair fish in the sea. An anyway," he shrugged as he headed off for the tunnel, "Ah'm Rovers through an through."

∗∗∗

It was a couple of days later that the letter came. Deano was late that morn, strolling through the changing room with his bag over his shoulder and an envelope held up at chest-height. He scrutinized it quizzically, like the wrong page of a road atlas, before holding it out to Johnny.

"Here, Johnny," he said, "This just came in for you."

"Ma hauns are a bit dirty," Johnny replied, trying not to look, "Could you just set it doon there?"

Deano shrugged, flicked it onto the bench and walked off. After a few moments of agonised *sang-froid*, Johnny picked up the letter and read it. As he reached its end, Deano glanced up casually from cleaning his boots.

"Zat your girlfriend, Johnny?" he asked.

"Naw, it's fae ma auld coach in Australia, askin me tae go back," Johnny said.

"Go back where? Cambuslang? That's the postmark."

"Aye, he sends the letters tae ma pal in Cambuslang, an he forwards them tae me. Nae point in giein him ma address, ah might be movin on before lang."

"Movin on where?" Deano asked. "Australia?"

"Naw, ah widnae go back there," Johnny said with a note of finality, "It's too crowded."

"Oh, aye, aye, ah've heard that," Deano responded, "An anyway, ye're just waitin fur the Rovers tae pick up on ye, eh?"

"Where'd ye hear that?" Johnny rose to his feet, crumpling up the envelope carefully. "Ah'm United man an boy." And he walked out holding the letter, unaware that in the artificial glare of the light, United's crest was instantly recognisable through the translucent paper.

Deano, oblivious, pulled his socks up over his shinguards. I tried to meet his gaze, but it was cast resolutely at the floor.

"I never knew United's offices were in Cambuslang," I said.

Deano got to his feet, pulling out the creases of his kit with abnormal care.

"Aye, the things ye never knew ye never knew, eh?" And he clattered out the door, stamping the dirt from his boots as he went.

***

Johnny was never going to make much of a hardman – that much was obvious – but the next week, with Deano sitting out his suspension in the stand, he made a decent enough go at it.

"That's ninety minutes, dead on," Deano glanced at his watch, looking up in time to see Johnny skip over a tackle, "Je-SUS! Changed days since last week, eh? He'd have flung himself on the deck like a wean that's just had their favourite dolly put in the attic."

With the referee still checking the time, Johnny blasted in a shot from the angle which hit both posts on its way in. He celebrated briefly, lifting a single arm into the air, then stared searchingly into the crowd for a moment before turning away.

"Who were ye lookin for at the end, there, pal?" Deano asked, clapping him on the back afterwards. "The Match of the Day cameras?"

"Naw, it's ma new goal celebration," Johnny said, "Ah mean, ah invented it, but they're daein it aw over the place noo."

"Well, ah'd pit a patent oot on it if ah were you," Deano smiled, rubbing his hands together, "Ye'll be celebratin plenty o goals this season."

***

He wasn't wrong. The only thing Johnny did more often that season than hit the net was stare longingly into the stands. Deano, on the other hand, hadn't scored a single goal to speak of, but prized every one of Johnny's strikes as if it was his own.

"Thirty-three goals in thirty-five games! *Fae midfield!*" Deano laughed, the sports page unfolded over his knees, "And no a penalty among them! If thae skinflints had brought in a couple mair good players, we might've won the league!"

"There's still the semis of the cup," I said.

"True enough, eh. We've *got* tae win it this year," he muttered, suddenly serious, "Next year he'll get poached an we'll be back tae square wan. It's got tae be this year. It's got tae be."

The days leading up the semi-final passed by in a whizz of publicity, old-timers stopping you in the street to tell you they remember the last time Thistle got to a cup final. Win bonuses were promised; family members struggled for tickets; Deano watched *Braveheart* every night for a week. And then, within half an hour of it starting, it was over, Johnny Fotheringham notching the quickest hat-trick in Cup history to kick off an hour-long party in the stands, stands so full that after each goal he scanned down through the faces in lines like a letter, the same old letter he flattened out on his knee in the changing room afterwards and claimed this time was from Reebok.

"It'd be a lot mair money," he admitted, "But a promise is a promise, an ah telt Hi-Tec ah'd stick wi them."

"They've done ye just fine the day, eh, pal?" Deano beamed in delight, drenched from head to toe in water and champagne.

"These auld things?" Johnny stared down glumly at them, "Ah'd have goat two hat-tricks if it wisnae fur them. Might as well be playin wi Kleenex boxes on my feet."

He read the letter once more, crumpled it up finally, and dropped it in the bin.

"Ach well." He looked thoughtful. "Ye live an learn."

***

Next week, Johnny had an absolutely shocker. Substituted after an hour, he walked off down the tunnel without a word. He'd plodded through the match like a weary toddler, twice refusing (at Deano's insistence) to take a penalty because "someone else should get a chance". The cup final was in a week's time. Deano was frantic.

"Ah tried tae make him take a penalty, just tae git his confidence up," he

108

moaned afterwards, his head in his hands, "But he willnae take them cos he's scared o lookin stupid if he misses. Whit's he gonnae be like in the cup final? Ma heid's mince here, by the way. United widnae touch him wi a bargepole, noo."

Just at that Johnny slunk into the changing room, fresh from the shower. Betraying no awareness of Deano's piercing stare, he picked up his kit bag and turned to leave.

"You're daein ma heid in here, Johnny," Deano burst out, "Whit's gaun oan? Is it yer boots? The baws? The grass no the right colour? Tell us whit it is, an whitever it is, we can fix it."

Johnny listened without looking, then shrugged his shoulders.

"Naw, it's no that," he answered quietly, "It's nothin like that. Ah guess ah'm just no playin very well."

And before anyone else could say anything, he was gone.

***

The cup final arrived with little fanfare. Without Johnny's goals or Deano's enthusiasm for them, the run-up had been miserable, the whole changing room sucked into the

109

silence that gaped between the two men. In blazers and club ties we boarded the bus, Johnny dazed, half-asleep, up the front, whilst Deano at the back twitched like a condemned man dreaming of the electric chair.

We worked our way through the day's rituals, eating and gladhanding, nodding politely at the stadium tour. The steep, empty stands rose like cliffs beside us. Deano, no matter who was talking or what we were doing, kept allowing his gaze to scramble up them, the blue and red rows which radiated out from the light, bright green. Johnny, on the other hand, had yet to lift his head even once from the turf, which he scanned intently, as if searching for clovers. We changed and went out to warm up. As we jogged through our desultory exercises, Deano took a glance, and then another glance, at the glass of the executive's box, high above.

"Here!" he said, pointing. "Izzat who ah think it is?"

I looked up. Sitting in the executive box, notepad out, eyes trained unmistakably on Johnny, was Gerry Lennox, the United scout.

Johnny's head shot up at the name in surprise. He stared up at the box, a smile briefly troubling his face before sinking beneath   insouciance.

110

"Auld Gerry," he said, "Ah telt him ah'd get him some good seats."

"Did you, Johnny?" I said. I glanced at Deano, but he was already turning away.

***

It was ten years later, after we'd retired, that Deano and I heard from Johnny again. He'd done well for himself, we knew that, but we couldn't get over the post-code on the letter inviting us round, never mind his house when we saw it.

"Nah, this is just ma holiday home, really," he told us when he came to the door, "Sorry aboot the mess 'n' that. Ah'm embarrassed aboot inviting ye roond, tae be honest. Tip like this. But ah've goat some stuff here ah thought ye might like tae see."

"Whit is it, the Ark o the Covenant?" Deano asked, peering around the lobby's many exits.

"Naw, the hoose is too wee," Johnny answered uncertainly, hanging our jackets up, "C'mon this way. It's good tae see ye baith, by the way. It's been a while."

We followed him as he showed us round the house, boasting apologetically about its myriad luxuries – the comfyness of the seats, the size of the TV.

"Sorry ah've no goat anythin better for you than this gutrot," he said in one room, pouring gold elixir from a decanter, "Ah'm hardly ever in, ye see."

"No thinkin o slowin doon a bit, Johnny?" Deano asked. "Ah mean, ye've no goat forever."

"Ach, the boy's got a few good years left in him," I said. "A few medals still to add to the collection, eh?"

He took a sip of his whiskey as we walked, and shrugged.

"Could be. Speakin of which…"

Johnny opened a door, turned on the lights. The room was huge, and glittering everywhere with glass cases and silver trophies. We looked around, Johnny modestly standing off to one side, next to a long glass cabinet full of medals.

"Ye've done well fur yersel, son, ah'll say that." Deano nodded in approval, his eyes glazed.

"Ah'd have twice the number o caps if it hadnae been fur that MacDonald eejit," Johnny sighed, "He couldnae manage a chip shop. But ah've done awright, ah suppose. Here, c'mon see these."

The cabinet was laid out in neat rows, medals daintily inscribed with the team and date and competition. *United, League Cup Winners, 08/09. United, Scottish Cup Winners, 05/06. United, Premier League Champions, 09/10.*

Deano smiled and pointed at one of the medals. It was small and dark as an old two pence. *Thistle,* it said. *Challenge Cup Runners-Up, 98/99.*

"God, Johnny, whit ye daein wi that, still? Half the taxi drivers in Airdrie have got yin!"

Johnny shrugged diffidently. "A medal's a medal, in't it?"

Deano stared at the medal again, as if in awe at the company it kept.

"Aye, it is that."

We walked on. Framed shirts lined the wall, bookshelves full of playing awards, a handful of old-fashioned caps with the names of the opponents on them in yellow – Finland, Cyprus, the Netherlands. The team photos showed an increasingly weathered Johnny standing on the outskirts, then the front, then finally the centre of the United squad.

"Ah'll probably wind up managin them, wan day," Johnny told us, "It'll be a while yet, but it's there if ah want it."

We finally reached the other end of the room, where Johnny held the door open for us. As I crossed through, Deano lingered for a moment behind me. He shook his unbelieving head over his whiskey, looked around one last time, and laughed.

"My god, Johnny! Ye're some boy." He ran his free hand through his greying hair. "Whit a room! Whit a life! Ah've no got many medals to tell ma weans aboot, but it's something, in't it, tae say ye've hiv played wi a United legend."

Johnny stared at him in confusion, and his face crinkled into an all-too-familiar frown.

"United legend? Och naw," he said, ushering us through, "Ah'm a Thistle man, masel."

The River of Silver

Everyone knew that in summer the road to Quilmes would grow as tropic as the jungle, and everything on it become a mirage. After the war, when the oil refineries started up again, the skies above Buenos Aires had turned green with smoke, and the surrounding network of capillary roads were choked with drum-heaped trucks. From then, things had gone from bad to worse, and nowadays even the silver ripples of the Rio de la Plata, which ran along the cliff-side road, were murky with the sky's reflected grime. It was far from the Argentina Juan Botasso had grown up in, before the war, before the revolution. Though given to fantastic gestures, he was not strictly speaking a political man, and neither of these events had meant much to him; as he squinted into the leaking wall of colours ahead he merely reflected on the pity of it, that he, *la arana negra*, should now need glasses just to ride his motorbike.

La arana negra, the Black Spider – that nickname had not stuck. In fact, he had not been called it in twenty years. The final had not been quite the hoop-la then that it later became – Juan did not kid himself – but there were those who said the first *coup* might never have happened if only

Argentina had won. It was not a notion which Juan was inclined to agree with ("Then perhaps *El Presidente* should have played in goals himself," he would caustically remark) but it did chime in certain aspects with his increasingly narrow view of his fellow man, and there were moments indeed when he found himself wondering. There had been no more World Cups after that, no more finals. Juan's runners-up medal was rumoured to lie at the bottom of the Rio Plata – children attributed to this belief the water's name, *the River of Silver* – but in fact he had sold it from necessity long ago. No, that was not true. Necessity had played no part. He had simply had enough.

On a clear day like today, as he climbed the cliffs and cut the evening smog, he could see all the way to Uruguay across the Rio; and yet it was not until the last moment that Juan spotted the darks trucks as they bulleted towards him, swinging the wheel of his bike towards the clifftop's edge. There had still been time to react – in split-seconds shorter than these he had thrown himself at impossible distance, turned thumping headers back into the sky – but he sat there, erect, watching as the dusty ground spooled out from under him, and the brawling rushes of the river reached up. Then the wheels of his Ducati were spinning impotently against the sky, and the grand capital of Uruguay sprung up from where it crouched on the other side of the river, like a beast that drank, the only point of reference for Juan as he struggled in the air.

Montevideo – *I see the mountain!* – where the final had been played, and was still played now, in the hilltops of men's dreams. As he scuttled across the invisible line of his goal, Juan Botasso wished desperately that when the brown ball (whose fleeting glimpses he followed from one place to another like rumours of gold) emerged next from the ruck of legs and boots and rolled-down socks, it would be flying towards him rather than away, the imperceptible whistle of its valve cutting through the air, its panels spinning in the artificial light. If a ball spun, it assured him that not only had the striker failed to catch it right, but also that the laws of physics had not been momentarily suspended, that the shot would not simply pass through his hands like water. But strikes hit perfectly, as this Castro's was, they didn't spin – they simply vacillated a little from side to side, like the point of a pen being scribbled in the air. Its stillness made it seem like the ball was getting bigger rather than closer, a dark gigantic sun eclipsing the countless eyes that ranged beneath it. There was silence.

The Argentinians had come expecting mischief, but the only trick the Uruguayans had was their football. What a joke that was! Against better teams there was a chance at least. You knew what they were trying to do. Take France, for instance. They always chose the correct pass, and the chance, and the instant to take it – with them, everyone was on the same page. But Uruguay, though! *Hijos de putas!* They just stumbled from one mishap to another. This volley from Castro, in the final minute; Juan had tensed and relaxed, tensed and relaxed so many times that his nerves were shot with waiting. Feet flat, he stood transfixed as the ball crawled through a maze of limbs. A clean shot from an unclean moment – it was the worst of every world.

But he could see its whole circumference at least, so there could be no deflections, no clumsy shins or shoulders to turn away its arc. If he was going the right way (and he thought he was, his studs biting into the dirt) the ball was his. Stamping with his right leg, he pushed away the ground below, his feet lifting gently from the grass. His flight would be momentary – even now his entire body, from the top of his stretching hand, curls accommodatingly for its return to earth, his hip presenting itself to buffer,

118

his bicep pressed, a cushion, to his head. And in the sky above the Rio de la Plata, Juan Botasso manages to right himself, set still the see-sawing horizon that lies ahead, with Montevideo in the centre and nothing beneath but silver silence.

Here in mid-air he is safe from all the harm that is rushing in to meet him – the russet sphere his hands claw agonisingly towards, the many-thousand stares from both sides of the river, open-mouthed, intook breaths about to come roaring out, the very earth itself, that gigantic moon, crashing up into his gut. His gaze travels up the wrinkled terrain of his sleeve, stripes like village roads dashing along its canyons to emerge at the wrist, his thumb and forefinger visible behind his arm. The shadows beneath are spilling everywhere, in all directions; and on the blank grey static of the Rio de la Plata, a single outstretched arm has cast the shadow of a spider, and each and every bird becomes a flock in flight.

A Stranger Here Myself

There were a lot of things about his new life that Patryk didn't understand, and the Glasgow Subway was one of them. Well, actually, he understood it full well, and this was what perturbed him. It was safe, and simple, and people used it to go places. This was not what he had been led to expect. There had not been a subway network in Poland, but he'd seen the American movies in the cinema, with their graffitied trainfuls of knives and roaming gangs, and even the Metro in Prague, it was said, had a dismal reputation. On Glasgow's Subway, however, he had seen nothing worse than the singing, staggering drunks, sucked into the open doors of the train like moths and expelled again a few stops later. It was a simple network, a single citywide oval, perfect for winos and foreigners. Once, when he had missed his stop, Patryk had stayed on the train for a whole clockwise circuit rather than get off and go back the way. He found the shabby gentility of the little orange carriages and their tiny ceramic stations soothing, appreciated the sedate pace of their limited life, with no kids or inspectors or hectoring announcements. As he rose to disembark, it occurred to him for the first time, and with a pang of jealousy, that the trains actually had drivers. That, he thought, he disapproved of. It hardly seemed necessary.

All Patryk was looking for was a quiet life. He didn't want any trouble, he had seen enough of that. He just wanted to be left alone to drink his coffee and read his books. It was difficult, to be sure, but he just about had the hang of it. There was a decent sized Polish diaspora in Scotland, and an bigger Slavic one, but the idea of that kind of forced intimacy with people who'd have passed him by without a glance in Krakow did not appeal to him. He had come to Scotland to get away from his family, not to acquire another. The Glaswegians, on the other hand, he avoided as much as possible, if only because there was a faintly intimidating edge to their friendliness which Patryk found more threatening than actual fury. Their laughter, when it came, was to him an intrusion, a playful punch to a hidden sore. He skulked behind the language barrier as much as possible, smiling and shrugging his shoulders – but some of the other builders did not mind that he pretended not to know English, scarcely even noticed it, and bantered the morning away like card-sharps with a customer. It reminded him of the way his father had used to talk to his grandparents' graves. *"I am Polish,"* he wanted to tell them, *"Not dead."* But, on the whole, the current arrangement suited him. The work was not easy, but the money was good. On Saturdays, when half the city was watching football, he'd head on down to Waterstones, buy the *Gazeta Wyborcza* and a café latte, and sit down for a read. It was his sole experiment in social interaction, and in a way it was not so very different from speaking to an ancestor's grave, a little gesture of respect for his old, dead homeland, and the one he lived in now.

As he perused the many-coloured pages of the foreign weeklies he noticed, with a sinking heart, that someone was looking at him. He glanced at them, quickly, then away. A man, a big man at that, with ginger hair and rusty stubble, was staring at him intently over a cup of tea. There had been something like surprise in that large, doughy face, a little of the wide eyes and open mouth which Patryk recognised from Hollywood films as meaning *You?! Here?!* He scanned up and down the newspaper rack in a quick pantomime of discernment, trying to work out what the man could mean. Debts? He didn't have any. Friends, none of those either. Or had the man just picked him out for a foreigner? Yes, it was possible. Patryk was small and pale, with twitchy eyes and dark hair. He did not need to have a copy of *Rzeczpospolita* under one arm for a xenophobe to mark him as Slavic.

Patryk glanced again at the newspapers, wondered if the pretence at another nationality might get him off the hook. Fingering the pink pages of the *Gazetta dello Sport*, he thought wistfully of an Italian Albanian he sometimes saw. It was strange how many people here did not seem to see racism against Slavs as being quite the same thing as, say, racism against Asians. The Bulgarians, they had it worst. They were really only here to earn money, an economic outlook most Glaswegians shared and understood, but others found unforgivable. When first visiting the public library Patryk had, as was his habit, taken a taxi from the train station rather than ask directions. During the course of the five minute journey the driver had told him, without irony, that Bulgarians were both scheming frauds raking in benefits and subhuman monsters raking through bins. Guiltily, Patryk had said he was Polish, to which the driver had responded with a cheerful story about some Poles he'd met at a football match; good lads they were, with a jug of home-made spirits so strong he'd felt it burn all the way to his stomach. Of course, not everybody understood the distinction between Poles and Bulgarians, or cared, and even making that distinction himself cost Patryk spiritually. After reaching the library, he had picked up a membership form, stared dully at the Slavic literature shelf, and walked back to the station.

He looked over at the chairs again, by accident. The man, still staring, fixed him with a knowing smile. That was it, Patryk thought. Time to go. He headed for the exit, skirting as far away from the man and his slowly revolving stare as was possible. Every part of him suddenly seemed fragile and uncontrollable, like he was a mannequin made of string and old cans. As he juddered his way out of the man's line of sight a voice, groaning and deep like a boat in the sea, called after him.

"Hoi, Lubo!"

Patryk staggered. He had heard this sort of thing already many times, Muslims passing by the building site caustically referred to as "Ahmed" or "Abdul". It had never happened to him before, although he'd always expected it to; and yet now that it had he couldn't quite believe it. He realised, suddenly, that no part of him had been ready for this, no matter how much he had prepared. Months, needless, miserable months he had spent steeling himself, flinching at every passing gaze – for nothing.

He stumbled on along the bookshelves, listening for the warning scrape of chair legs on the floor. The fluorescent heat grew overpowering. At each step his toes snagged mysteriously on the floor, as if the dank carpet had suddenly grown cognizant of his fear and was grasping at him. Shop clerks with black shirts stared through their spectacles, voicing things he couldn't understand. Somehow, he felt more at risk in this storeful of strangers than he would have in the street. If he could only get outside, he thought, he would be safe.

On through the strange syllables and children's cries he staggered, everywhere the books burning in his eyes, the glass beaming down. A vicious maze of corduroy, baskets, and floral prints balked him, forming and reforming, enveloping him with their soft admonishments. The world, at once, was muggy and unreal, a shadow cast by a furious sun; and he was a mote, a bubble sinking in the heavy air, a small void struggling towards a larger one.

He reached the glass doors and plunged through them. The warmth of the pulsing air was no respite, and touched his heart like tinder. In the street outside, people who did not know him walked back and forth, oblivious. This was no escape. He turned back. Sure enough, there he was, the man, pushing open the door with one solid swing of his arm, every muscle coiled like purpose.

"Hoi. Lubo."

Patryk stared wildly around him, unable yet to believe that it had happened, or was about to. A street artist juggled a football nearby, to the envious applause of countless watchers. The man stepped forward. Patryk realised that he had not breathed in several seconds, and had not even strength to scream when the huge hand shot out at him, flourishing a newspaper under his nose. On its back page a small, pale, dark-haired man with twitchy eyes held his arms aloft in triumph; on all sides of him erupted a delirious legion of green and white. Behind, still bouncing, a ball was nestled in an empty net. The man fumbled in his pocket and eventually pulled out a pen with a mute little gesture of writing.

"Lubo. Sign please?"

Black Sheep

It was Alan's turn to choose the music this week. The rest of the lads had been out the night before, but Alan had stayed at home working on his mix tape. The last song on it was *The Boys Are Back in Town*, and he was determined that it should be playing as they pulled up at the ground. After calibrating the tape to match the length of their journey he'd slapped it into the car's tape deck and set out on a test run, stopping by all the usual pick-up points before wheeling into the deserted car park. As the car stopped outside the changing rooms, its headlights rocked from side to side and settled, cutting a dull slice of light into the dark grid of pitches. Twelve hours left till kick-off. Alan crouched over the steering wheel and stared. He hoped that he'd be able to sleep.

The following morning, when Alan went to pick them up, Niall and Paul were there on time, but Stevie was late and grumbling about a headache. Gregor, who was next, came from a neighbourhood which bordered on the ritzy, and the street they waited for him on was fringed with lilac roses and hand-waxed cars. Stevie squinted at the tape deck and rubbed his head.

"Is this Phil Collins?" he asked accusingly. Alan drummed his fingers urgently on the steering wheel.

"Genesis," he said.

They were already two songs behind schedule when the front door opened and Mrs. Cumming doddered up the path to tell them Gregor couldn't play. Alan, who was normally a very careful driver, put his foot to the floor and gritted his teeth, willing the bus stops to flash by faster – but it was all in vain, and the tape had snapped off long before they reached the car park. In silence they trundled across the tarmac and stopped in front of the changing rooms.

Shaz, as usual, was already there. He wore a knock-off Brazil shirt and old jogging trousers which were immaculately pressed, and was busy picking leaves off the hood of his car. It was an impossible task – the trees were directly overhead - but it gave him something to do.

"How come Shaz always wears joggies?" Stevie asked, tugging at his jammed seatbelt, "I'm no being funny, but is it a religious thing or is he just that shy?"

"Ehh, I don't think it's his religion. That other boy, Feisal, he never wears them," Paul said.

"We could do with *him* playing for us, I'll tell you," Stevie muttered, "Shaz is, like, the third-worst player I've ever seen… Well hullo there Shaz! How's it hanging?"

A smile writhed uncertainly on Shaz's face. He pushed his glasses back up his nose with his index finger. He was never seen without them, not even at fives.

"Got your money?" Alan asked. Shaz nodded and held out an upturned fist. Its contents poured noisily into Alan's cupped hands.

"Jeez oh! Talk aboot cross my palms with silver, eh?" Stevie grimaced, "That all from your dad's shop?"

Alan poked a suspicious finger through the piled-up coppers.

"That's only two pounds, Shaz," he said, "It's two pounds if there's six of us. Gregor's not coming. It's two-fifty."

Shaz smiled apologetically. Alan looked at them.

"Well, what're we going to do? It's two-fift…"

"Och, *here*," Stevie cut in, grabbing Alan's hand and jamming a fifty pee in it, "And don't bother paying us back, Shaz. I've no use for it in bawbees, or ginger bottles, or whatever." He

130

stuck his wallet back in his rucksack and let it swing by a single strap from his hand, winding and unwinding in the breeze.

On the pitches behind them the ten o'clock matches had finished up, and the teams were heading back in. Some were dressed in identical kits, entire squads that sported store-bought Celtic shirts; other groups were rag-tag; most, like the Heidless Chickens themselves, were loosely based around a pastel theme. Shaz's Brazil shirt had only been through the wash once but had faded badly, and its hue now merely suggested yellow, like a lemon ice-lolly melting in the heat. Stevie's Jamaica shirt was vibrant neon; Niall and Alan, the dingy amber of Motherwell strips gone by. Paul, despite not being the goalkeeper, had on a goalie top with black padded shoulders. They always arrived already changed, apprehensive somehow of the communal locker room, and as they clustered around the fixture list only Niall sat apart, putting on his gloves.

"Here we go, then," Alan read, running his finger along the plastic-covered notice board, "Division 5, Pitch 6, Bayer Leverboozin versus…" his snub nose wrinkled in disgust, "*The Heidless Chickens.*"

"Great name," Stevie muttered indistinctly. He had pulled the collar of his shirt up over his nose, and was absently chewing its bobbled polyester.

"We're changing it next season," Alan scowled, "You any idea how that affects our morale? Makes us look like a right bunch of idiots…"

"Say that again," Stevie said.

Alan fell silent again. Stevie clapped his hands together, parcelled out a few smiles as if they were survival rations.

"We up for this the day, lads? How's about it, Shaz, we up for this? MON THE CHICKENS!"

They crept behind him in single file along the narrow path. There were twelve pitches, back-to-back in rows of six, all about the size of a tennis court. Each pitch was separated from the others by heavy wooden boards, dark green and spackled with graffiti. At about shoulder-height the boards turned into loose, twiny nets, held up at every corner of the pitch by a single spindly floodlight. The goals at both ends of the pitch were long rather than tall, and the Astroturf itself was little more than cheap green carpet; as Alan walked out onto it, and booted his ball into the net, his lime-green boots sent forth a wave of sand. Stevie shielded his   eyes.

"Hoi, referee sir, how's yer eyesight the day?"

The referee ambled along the pitch with a weary smile. As Stevie went over to speak to him, the Heidless Chickens formed a loose shape and kicked the ball around.

"There's five past, ref. They're no here by ten past…"

"*Quarter* past."

"Oh, is it quarter past now?" As he walked back towards them, Stevie kicked out his legs in cursory warm-up. "Nae odds to me. We could stick till midnight and they still widnae show."

"Sunday morning hangover?" Paul said.

"Aye, so it is! They're ducking us. Just as well," Stevie dusted his hands off significantly, "Otherwise it'd be *that*, I'm telling you. Child's play. Like…"

The entire pitch shook as the door, a heavy gate of latticed metal, was flung open. The men were fat and thirty-something, and their strips were black and white. Their bleary eyes were fixed ahead, and their faces prickled with ginger stubble.

"You Bayer Leverboozin?" the ref asked.

Someone grunted. Sullenly they began to whang their heavy ball around, thumping it towards the net and anything else nearby. Behind the goal, a man in a navy tracksuit cursed joylessly at them between draughts from a dark green bottle. After screwing the lid back on tight, the man laid the bottle carefully on its side, pulled on a pair of goalie gloves – cheap ones, made of orange wool, with patches of black rubber stitched here and there across their palms – and took up position in the net. Stevie glanced around at his teammates and winked.

"Poundland gloves, Poundland goalie," he whispered, "Men against boys, this."

Finally, the referee blew his whistle and motioned both captains to the middle. It was Alan's turn this week, but he checked with Stevie anyway, who nodded him on. The other team didn't seem to have a captain, or any player identifiably different from the others – the man standing opposite was just the nearest player to the middle.

"Heids or tails?" the ref asked.

"Heads," said Alan.

Heads it was. Alan winced apologetically and smiled at his silently chewing opponent, who stared past him into the distance.

"We'll take kick-off," the man croaked.

Alan glanced over at Stevie, who didn't seem to have noticed.

"Okay," he said, "We'll take the half."

He extended his hand to the other player, who glanced down, hawked noisily into his open fist, and stuck out his palm. Alan's gaze climbed blankly from the man's knobbly hand to his face and back again. The other lad snorted and turned away; his hand left a slug-trail down his shorts where he wiped it.

"Let's get intae this lot, eh?" Stevie shouted, "MON THE CHICKENS!"

By now the games on all the other pitches had long since kicked off, and the additional clamour of one more match was nothing. A quick one-two set Alan free, and he toe-ended the ball into the far corner of the net.

"Candy from a baby, wee man!" Stevie smiled, his palm uplifted. Alan, who was apt to miss high-fives, lifted his open hand and pressed it carefully against his teammate's. Stevie turned away and clapped his hands.

"There for the taking, boys!" he shouted, "Winners, right, winners all the way!"

But Bayer Leverboozin were hard to knock off the ball once they'd got it, and they fought for everything. One-nil became one-all, then two, then three. When their fourth goal went through Niall's hands and clanged in via the hollow post, Stevie picked up the ball and turned slowly away from the scene of the disaster, his arms spread out in temporarily mute appeal.

"Track the fuck back, Alan!" he shouted, "Who're you supposed to be marking?"

Alan, who was walking back from the other half, looked up.

"Ehm, I was picking up the guy with the…"

Stevie slammed the ball down on the ground and stormed away muttering.

By half-time they were already 5-1 down. As they huddled behind their own goal with bottles of Lucozade, Stevie stared levelly at Alan, waiting for him to say something.

"Well…"

"Paul's on *him* and Shaz is on *him* and I'm on *him*," Stevie burst in, gouging marks in the sand with his toe, "So where does that leave you, Alan? What are you doing?"

"I'm picking up the spare   man."

"Aye, the spare – until he makes a run," Stevie said, "Then you'd be as well no playing. Marking somebody's no the same as just *watching* them."

"Well," Alan swallowed, "I score most of the goals, so I feel like that's me doing my bit."

"You score the g... One toe-bash and that's you clocking oot for the day, is it? That's how it works?"

"Well, it wasn't a toe-bash, it was a sidefoot, and..."

"Listen, *you*," Stevie's blue eyes went dead in his face. "It was a fucking TB and there's nae buts aboot it. If you want special treatment cause of your goalscoring, start scoring some fucking goals. Fuck *me*."

The second-half kicked off, and they conceded again almost straight away, but Stevie barged through to pull one back. Then Shaz tapped one in and Alan volleyed cleanly and suddenly it was 6-4.

"Brilliant, lads, let's keep this going!" Stevie shouted. Leverboozin were wilting visibly in the sun, their tired tackles falling short, their hands resting on their knees. There were ten minutes to go when Alan ran onto his own through ball and slung it past the goalie.

"Great feet, Alan, great feet!" Stevie slapped him on the back. "Keep it going wee man, that's the stuff!"

The men, they were finished. One of their players had retired permanently now, a wobbling mass crouched tragically behind the goal. They kicked and tackled and tried to break, but they had no legs left, and an over-hit pass sent the ball into the corner. Stevie doubled back to collect it, looked up. Ahead of him, the view had become static, a lush green bowling alley decorated with black and yellow pins. Across the silence, right in front of goal, Alan dashed, his bony arm extended, his finger pointing. Stevie clubbed his foot at the ball. It skipped up from off the Astro as if it were water, collided with the path of Alan's run. Then, like a thrown playing-card, it wobbled gently into the net.

"Handbaw!" shouted one, then all of the Leverboozin players. Alan, walking towards his own half, glanced back over his shoulder, then quickly down at the ground. The referee made a mark in his notebook and put it away.

"Six each," he said.

"You fuckin…"

Everyone stared as the biggest of the Leverboozin players rushed straight towards

138

the referee. His entire shaven head was dark maroon, the crumpled remnants of an unfired pot, with staring eyes that were folded in his face like pearls inside a mollusc.

"Handbaw! That was fuckin handbaw! You blind or something? That wee prick's been getting away with everything in this game! Aye, fuck you, ref, fuck your red card, fuck it." As the referee tugged his red card shakily from his pocket, the big man slapped it from his hand.

"You can get tae fuck, ya knob-end. And *you*," he turned and pointed at Alan, his tattooed arm shooting out from its sleeve, "You mouthy wee poof. I'll be waiting for you."

As he stormed off the pitch he slammed the metal gate hard behind him, and the entire frame of the pitch whistled and shook like wires in the wind. The other games had all ended by now, and the only sound to be heard was the rattle of departing cars crunching across the asphalt.

"Okay, lads," the referee said in a strained voice, "Kick off. Six each."

A man came scowling up to centre, slammed the ball down with one massive paw, and lashed it towards Alan as hard as he could. Alan yelped and ducked. The ball hurtled past and smashed against the boards.

"Free kick," said the ref.

Stevie looked at him in dismay.

"Referee, man…"

The referee's face went hard.

"You've got the free-kick, son. What else am I supposed to do?"

Stevie glanced at the other side of the pitch, where the four remaining men in black stared at them malignantly, then walked over to the ball. Alan's palms were open in front of his chest, and his eyes were barren.

"This isnae worth it, Alan," Stevie hissed, "On you go, sneak away and get up the road. Don't wait for us. We'll play with four, it'll no matter." Alan's face was immobile. "Alan, it'll no matter, I said. Just on you go."

Alan still didn't say anything. Across the field, against a backdrop of empty courts, the Leverboozin players fixed their eyes on his, and panted silently.

"Just fucking get on with it," one of them said.

Stevie turned to the   Chickens.

"Don't pass to Alan, right? It's four on four now. We're playing without him. *Black sheep.*"

Alan, who still hadn't moved, watched blankly as his teammates moved up field, breaking around him like waves around a rock. *Black sheep.* That's what they'd called them, the big boys, kids who were too fragile to be passed to or tackled. Up in the long, wall-length window of the clubhouse, its big screen showing the big game, all heads were turned away. Alan heard the heavy ball hit the pitchside board, wondered which of his team-mates had missed the shot; then, a moment later, they rushed back past him in a series of black shadows and yellow flashes, like sunlight bursting through the trees.

"He's mine, Shaz! GO TO HIM!" Stevie roared. Niall, diving, pulled his knees up to his chest, and a shot richocheted against them. High in the air it spun, back through the advancing waves, and rolled out towards the pitch's centre.

"LEAVE IT, ALAN!" Stevie shouted, desperately swimming against his own momentum.

As he collected the ball and turned past the halfway line, there was so much ahead of Alan still to go, so much time left to think, and he tried to focus it all on one tiny square of the net, not on the screaming and shouting, the stampede of boots, the brutish little goalkeeper scurrying wickedly towards him – or beyond that, the field, the trees, the houses, the happy people in them – all of them silent and still with watching. One yard after another slipped past into the void that trampled up behind him, the ball luring him further and further on. He drew back his foot. There could be no losing it now. From here on it would be winners, winners all the way.

Disgrace

The light in the medical room is flickering badly. Like most rooms at Recreation Park it is rarely used, and then only for purposes of storage; the sole concession to its nominal purpose is a sign on the door and a rickety medical table in the middle of the room. A single figure is sitting on it now, bent double at the waist, its short limbs hanging down like a rag doll whose stuffing has collected at the ends. Around it, in amongst the footballing bric-a-brac, half-a-dozen figures storm around in various attitudes of despair, disgust and fury. It is bedlam, fucking bedlam. Who can believe it? A fat man stands by the impenetrable murk of the window, a sliver of mobile phone pressed more to his mouth than his ear. He swivels his eyes around. There's some serious economy of movement going on there. You get the idea even his head would have the turning circle of an aircraft carrier.

"Hello, polis?" His voice is shaking like a bridge in a high wind. "Izzat the polis? One o oor committee's been attacked. Can ye send somebody doon straight away?" The wee fella close to him looks up. He is on his eighth circuit of the room already, and they've only been in there five minutes. He looks right at home, stamping around the subterranean dark like Rumpelstiltskin about to start spinning gold.

"That's no right, that. That's no fuckin right. They're guests at oor club. They cannae get away wi it. It's a disgrace, so it is." He slams his fist into his open palm. "Somebody needs tae get up there an sort them aw oot. They're probably up there right now trashin the place."

"Too right!" This other lad is tall, with a beaky nose and great white wings of hair, like a totem pole. "It's not on. Ye cannae go marchin intae somebody else's clubrooms an then… Whit's it he hit him wi? A chair?"

"A table," says the wee man.

"Fuck me! A table?! Whit, wan o the wee yins?"

"Naw, that big one up at the kitchen."

The tall lad looks around.

"Jeez oh. Anybody phonin an ambulance?"

"Aye, Chappy's on the phone the noo." Chappy, in the opposite corner, holds up a slab-like hand in acknowledgement.

"Hiya, can we get an ambulance sent oot tae Recreation Park? We've had a boy get the malky put on him. Total GBH like. Nae fuckin need."

"A table. Ah cannae fuckin get over this," the wee man says.

"Eh? Aye, hit him with a table," Chappy says into the phone. He pauses and scratches his ear with a ring-barnacled finger. "Naw, he never picked the table up, just belted him in the face, then smashed him heid-first intae it. Ye're needin to get somethin done aboot it. It's a bloody disgrace."

The wee man sets his jaw impressively.

"Ah'd like tae see them try that on *me*. There'd be fuckin Tokyo, nae kiddin." The tall man nods in vigorous assent.

"Ah'll tell ye whit, though, ah'm no going back oot there until they bastards are away. If wan o them was to walk in here the noo, ah don't think ah could control masel. There'd be bloodshed, ah'm tellin ye."

Chappy is facing the other way now, idling with the door of a long disused cabinet.

"Aye, he's in a right bad way. Ye can take it from me, if ma son-in-law was here an saw that, it widnae be an ambulance ye'd be sendin, it would be a bloody Pickfords truck. Eh, whit?" Chappy frowns. "Is he breathin?"

He turns to the body on the table, a motionless mound emitting deep, racking rasps of air.

"Aye," he says, "Jist aboot. It's a fuckin sin, so it is. When's that ambulance gonnae git here then, eh? Ye're wantin to take a look at yersels."

He listens for a moment, thumping himself down on the edge of the medical table, which seems to stay together by dint of surface tension alone.

"Aye, well, that's what you call it. Me, ah call it a fuckin disgrace."

***

"Where's the rest o them, then?"

The clubroom is empty but for two men with black and yellow ties, sitting at a table. They have just been joined by a loose-faced little bulldog of a man, snaking his way between the pool table and the jukebox. He has rolled a match programme up into a truncheon, and is drumming it quickly on the back of a chair.

"Not a clue," he says, "There's no even anybody in the toilet. Saw that wee fat

146

bastard with the lisp five minutes ago, but he hit his leg on the table an near enough burst oot greetin. D'ye want me tae go look for them?"

"Nah. Forget it." The taller of the two men gets up, brushes some crumbs from his suit. "Let's just head. This is nae way to treat anybody. We're guests here, ye know."

The other man picks up a folder from an adjacent chair and hauls himself upright. The three of them take one last look around the deserted clubrooms. The paper plates, the beans on the boil, the empty bar with the sink still running, all of it like a surprise party waiting to happen. The bulldog's face sinks even further in fleshy repose.

"Talk aboot bad losers! Ye widnae treat yer worst enemy like that, would ye? Fitba's fitba, but some folk just take it too far. Nae wonder they're the laughin stock o the league."

The taller man shakes his head, lifts his keys from the table. He turns towards the door.

"Ah'll tell ye whit, though," he says, "It's a fuckin disgrace."

Slave Labour

Ach, it was a cushy number at the civic centre alright, and you'd get no argument from Wee Peter about that. I mean, think about it; all he did was take the money in and give them a chap on the window at when their hour was up. A chimp could do it. Didn't even have to put the goals up or anything, that was all done for him. Money for old rope or what? Fair enough, he'd had to phone an ambulance once when someone broke their leg. That could've been stressful. But once he'd done, it was back to the wee office; blinds down, kettle on, Sportscene on the radio. Nope. Sorry, boys, (he'd yawn with a luxurious stretch of his arms) it's not exactly six months hard labour. A bit of hard work never killed anyone, but why take the risk?

A man'd come round from the council once, checking on caretaker workloads. *That* soon set his gas at a peep, Peter chuckled to himself. He remembered the lad phoning HQ, telling his boss there was a guy here who was basically getting paid for not stealing any money. Wee Peter's professional integrity had been stung by this inference, for he proudly regarded every last penny he made as stolen. The idea that anything he owned had been honestly come by was a brazen affront to his self-image, and only his fear of the probable consequences had prevented him from saying so. Actual theft – well, that was just a little too much trouble to go to, but Wee Peter possessed some of the dignity of the amateur, and hated to be seen as a mere dabbler. Truth be told, if 99% of professionalism consisted of jargon, as many held it did, then Wee Peter would have been a world authority on the professionalism of the non-profession, a fully paid-up member of the chartered layabouts. "If Wee Peter put as much effort into daein work as he puts into dodging it, he'd be a multimillionaire." Nobody had ever actually said this, but Peter was determined that, some day, somebody should. He spent much of his time in the pub trying to generate this kind of shopfloor buzz for himself, huge handfuls of ironic self-deprecation cast around like breadcrumbs.

"Nothing like a pint efter a hard day's work, eh?"

"Maist exercise ah've had aw day!"

"Well, back tae the old grindstone… Ah don't think!"

There were rarely any takers, but these things took time. Jimmy had been going on about his angina for six months before anybody noticed, and even then it was because he'd collapsed on his way to the puggy. It wasn't that simple. There was groundwork to be laid. Rome wasn't built in a day, eh?

It was a different story at work, of course. Although Peter took a keen interest in the punters who came to use the games hall, he rarely saw them as effective targets for his banter. The paying customer, he shrewdly assessed, derived little pleasure from news of Peter's implied shiftlessness, and since that was all he was interested in talking about a conversational impasse could be very quickly reached. But he did get a kind of pleasure out of correctly remembering which group was due in next, and congratulated himself on his aptitude for spotting unusual celebrity likenesses. "Oh aye, there goes Steven Seagal." he'd say to himself, or "Dennis Taylor's late the day." The group currently assembling at the door, a bunch of students who played every Tuesday at 7pm, did not afford him much satisfaction in this line. He just took their money from them, always handed to him in a sweaty clump of change, and left them to get on with it. Only this time, he noticed with something like interest, they seemed to have brought their little brothers with them.

"Aye, well, you're the wan that's supposed tae've booked it." The voice occupied the aural hinterland that lies just before shouting. "Go ask him whit the score is."

Wee Peter shifted to the doorway. The lad who was speaking was one who he'd silently dubbed Cagney, a fizzy wee guy with a boyish face and a fearful temper. One week out of five he stormed off early, slamming the front door shut on a silence from which nothing fruitful ever grew. Today he stood apart, hands on hips, a loose corner of his vintage Scotland shirt dangling over his shorts. Behind him, the old blue pinboard advertised karate classes, Tae Kwon Do, fitness fads long forgotten. A smiley face made out of drawing pins looked on as Cagney noticed Wee Peter glancingly, and pointed over at him.

"There. There ye go. Ask him."

The player thus addressed was a tall lad, with blocky yellow boots that looked like they'd been hacked out of Polystyrene, and a careful centre-parting. His skin was so pale and taut he looked like a corpse that had forgotten to lie down. Minty, the others called him. He turned towards Peter, his beady little eyes showing nothing but pupil.

"We've got this booking," he said blankly, "We've got it every week."

From the doorway, Peter glanced at the wall planner. It was true enough, they did have it every week. But the name on the booking...

"Says here it's booked for Gallagher, that right?"

A wee lad in a Rangers top, maybe ten or eleven years old, piped up. His friends had assembled carefully behind him, peeping out on either side like a staged picture for a record sleeve.

"That's my da's name. He booked it for us."

Wee Peter looked at Minty. So, he noticed, did Cagney. Minty's hands hung limply by his side; he stared straight ahead.

"Aye, but my name's Craig."

"You better be kiddin," Cagney said. Wee Peter glanced again at the wall planner.

"Well, that's no the name oan the chart," he said carefully, "Ah mean, ah know you're here normally, but that's no the name oan the chart."

"Aye but, we book it every week," Minty said.

"Ah know." Wee Peter, skewered by the unblinking reptilian stare, started treading water. "But it says here it's booked by Gallagher, and this wee boy says he's Gallagher, so…"

"You're a fuckin… Sorry, lads," Cagney held an apologetic hand up to the logjam of boys in the hallway. He cranked his voice steadily up, one ratchet per sentence. "Ah telt ye tae phone an let them know we wurnae comin last week, so they widnae cancel the bookin fur this week. Ah telt ye, din't ah? Din't ah?"

"Aye but," Minty said, still staring straight through Peter's right shoulder, "We've got this booked. Every week." Peter looked at the wall chart again. His head was beginning to hurt.

"Well, thing is, these boys have got it booked this week. Ah mean, ah could always book it fur ye again fur next week, but this week… Ah mean, could ye's mebbe no share?" Cagney's face twisted into fierce contempt.

"Share?! Wi ten year aulds? Sorry, boys." The hand went up again. "These lads've goat it booked fair 'n' square. That's the way it is. Man up, you."

"Aye but," Minty said slowly, "We've got it booked."

"See if you say that again, swear tae God ah'm gonnae burst you."

Wee Peter still hovered in the doorway like a broken moth. His head felt like it was trapped in a vice. This was the longest he'd spent on his feet since 1987. He couldn't even manage to avoid Minty's gaze as it listed randomly around the room. His lungs felt frozen, suspended in the everlastingness of the moment. He took a deep, hiccupping breath, forced a sentence out like his body was a toothpaste tube with the cap still on.

"It's jist that…. Well, these boys have goat the booking the day. Ah mean, if ye come back next week, ah'll make sure ye're definitely back oan fur then. But this week, ah don't really think ah kin let ye oan…"

"Aye but," The words cut through his insides like the juddering of a meat thresher, "How no'?"

Cagney exploded like a cartoon bomb.

"*That's* how the fuck no!" he shouted, skelping Minty on the back of the head as he stormed out. The others followed, one by one. Peter watched them go, leaning against the frame of the doorway with the easy articulation of a Poundland action figure, until only Minty remained, dangling there like a carcass on a butcher's hook.

"Sorry aboot that, pal," Peter said, "Ah'll make sure it's aw sorted fur next week, eh."

He tilted thankfully around to his seat. Office surplus, it had never looked so comfy. The kettle had gone cold, but he would enjoy warming it up again. He imagined holding his face over his steaming mug, the tiny hammers on either side of his temple dissolving in the heat. Nearby lay the biscuit tin, and the open newspaper sprawled in exciting rumples of speculation. He swung the office door lazily shut behind him. It made a dull, rubbery *bong!* and swung back open. Peter stared down at the impeding obstacle. It was blocky, yellow, and looked as if it was made out of Polystyrene. From out of the living a dead voice spoke, and slithered awfully, like a slug-trail, into the labyrinth of his dreams.

"Aye but… we've booked it… we've always booked it…"

Bad News

It could be said that Jimmy Mitchell was not so very bad. Indeed, the committee had often said much the same thing themselves. He was a good family man, a trier, a doer of unpopular but occasionally necessary deeds. But now he had gone too far, and they'd decided they had to kill him.

It was the first committee meeting they had ever held without him, and as they sat in a semi-circle around the faux-pine table Jimmy's absence pulsed dully like an extracted tooth. Each space between them seemed subconsciously shaped to fit his ample bottom. Charlie coughed uneasily, reading and rereading the muddled agenda he had scribbled on a torn envelope. He turned it round in his hand, flattened it out, squinted at it, waiting for something to turn up. They were always waiting for something to turn up.

"Well? Whit's the crack, then?" said Wullie. "Are we gonnae get started, Mr. Chairman?" Wullie was a jovial, bear-like man, with a smile that jutted out his bottom jaw. He leaned over and gave Charlie a nudge with his elbow. Charlie rubbed his arms with paint-speckled fingers.

"Well, if we're no waitin for anybody else, we might as well make a start." He glanced around. "Does anybody know anybody who's no comin?"

"Aye." Stevie, thin and tall, hands folded behind his head, back so stiff it looked like a workman had propped him up against the chair and forgotten to pick him up again. He smiled an enigmatic v-shape. "Ian's pickin his boy up fae the Beebees. Says he'll try and make it alang efter that."

"Awright. Half-a-dozen's enough tae be gettin on." The light fuzzed in its plastic overhead. Someone had economically left off all the other lights in the clubroom, so that the long rectangle disappeared into darkness in both directions. An old pool table marked the edges of unstrained visibility. Charlie swivelled around in his seat to look at it.

"That pool table's a pure waste. Whit's-is-face… The boy who put it in…"

"Rocky," Wullie prompted.

"Aye, Rocky, he says he might as well take it away if it's no makin any money. He only goat thirty quid oot it the last time."

157

"Here!" Ally sat up, his blue eyes flashing open like a doll, "That cannae be right! They wee lads, ah see them playing it every week!"

"Who?"

"Och, ye ken them," Ally fluffed his white hair and stared at them monolithically, an Easter Island statue topped with birdshit. "Kenny's laddie and his pals."

"Aye, but are they payin for it?" Stevie nodded sagely to himself and turned his eyes up to the ceiling. A knowing grin settled on his face, like he had all the answers to the world's problems. Charlie silently unravelled this clue like a threadbare sweater.

"Whit! Is somebody giein them it for free?" His anxious gaze dashed around the table. "How can they be gittin it for free?"

Big Wullie stretched his arms out in a pantomime of casualness and checked an imaginary watch.

"Well, ma tea's waitin for me, so any chance we can get on to the matter at hand?"

"Aye, aye." Charlie tried to shuffle the papers in front of him before realising he only had one. "Right. We've called this meeting the

158

night tae talk aboot Jimmy."

Ally struggled up in his chair. "Well, ah think…"

Wullie half-raised his flat hand from the table like a drawbridge. "*Ah* think all discussion should go through the chairman." He settled back in his seat, interlocking his hands over his shirted stomach. "Mind, that's only wan man's opinion."

Ally nodded. "Aye, right enough. On ye go, Charlie."

Charlie chucked the agenda onto the table, trying to dismiss it.

"Right. So, you aw ken Jimmy's been makin an awfy lot of mistakes lately. He forgot tae register Davies fur the Scottish Cup — that cost us two grand…"

"Aye, AND got us chucked oot," Ally lamented.

"Aye, and that… And there was that business wi the minute's silence…"

They winced in collective recollection.

"Daftie told half them it was a minute's applause," Ally muttered, still stunned. Charlie nodded.

"Aye, then when we calmed everybody doon an Mrs. Dorricott had stopped   greetin…"

They had tried again for the minute's silence. Forty-five seconds of it had elapsed when Jimmy's wife had stuck her head out of the clubroom door.

Jimmy! Jimmy! We're aw oot of sausage rolls!

The seismic might of Jimmy's head lashing up from his mobile phone had carried all the way through his body, snapping him up onto his stubby little legs with an almighty bellow.

AGGIE! KIN YE NO SEE WUR HIVVIN A MINUTE'S SILENCE!

They sat there in expressive silence, the memory of that moment settling around them like dust. Charlie bounced his hand on his knee thoughtfully.

"Aye, so there's that. And then there's yon time wi the molehills…"

"The lawnmower parts…"

"The toilet door…"

"The insurance…"

For several minutes they passed Jimmy Mitchell's name round like a gigantic parcel of grievance, each torn layer revealing a fresh one, a semi-operatic lament of tragedies, dodgy dealings, good works become undone. A misshapen idol had arisen in the litany, dark handfuls of mud which merged into a bipedal lump.

"It's no even that that bothers me," Ally said, cutting off all previous discussion with a swipe of his hand. "Ah'm no fashed aboot him makin us look like a laughing stock, or aw the money he costs us. Whit does ma heid in is how he sidles up tae ye efter it, wi that stupit wee grin oan his face, and tells ye there's been *bad news*! Zif it's nowt tae dae wi him!"

They murmured in recognition. It was a pre-emptive wake, remembering him as if he was already dead, waddling across the beer-stained carpet with an opened letter in his hand and reverent glee on his face. "It's fae the S.F.A… It's fae the cooncil… Ah don't know if ah should tell ye… It's no very good news at aw…"

Wullie's voice came from so deep a place that you couldn't imagine it started inside him. When he opened his mouth, it was like the echoes of prehistory.

"Right, we already know aboot aw that. Question is, whit are we gonnae dae aboot it? There's nae point daein anythin else wi the club till we get him oot the door." There was a pause. "We've tried shuttin him oot, we've

161

tried forcin him oot, we've tried gettin him to resign. Nothin's worked. We're aw agreed oan that?"

"Without a doubt." Ally nodded over his folded arms.

"Right. Somebody's put it tae the committee — an ah dinnae ken who it wis — that we should just kill him. Noo, ah don't know how everybody feels aboot that. But, tae ma mind, unless somebody else has got a better idea, we might as well talk aboot it." Wullie gave a tiny shrug of his giant shoulders. "Fair enough. It might turn oot no tae be practical. But it costs nuthin tae talk aboot it." He settled back into his seat like a rock being rolled over the entrance to a cave. "Noo, ah'll be honest wae ye — ah think it's probably a bit o a last resort. But maybe that's where we've got tae. Whit does everybody else think? Sorry, Mr. Chairman." Wullie gave a little bow of mock deference and rolled his shoulders towards Charlie.

The chairman blew his reddened cheeks out and gazed round.

"Well. First things first. Ah mean, whit would we be talkin aboot daein here? Likesay, would we be daein it ourselves, or gettin somebody else in tae dae it for us? Whit do you think, Robbie?"

Robbie wriggled in his seat wordlessly, trying to free up a logjam in his oesophagus. He was fat and pale, as if he had been inexpertly carved from lard, with milky blond curls sprouting from his head like grass from a potato.

"Ah-ah-ah think it's somethin we definitely need tae have a wee think aboot. Ah mean, ah know he does his best, but whit else can we dae? Ah-ah-ah don't think WE should be daein it, though, just tae save a few bob. It's just gonnae wind up costin us mair in the long run, like when Ian and Wullie tried to put in that radiator."

Wullie laughed. "Aye, ah had ma eyes opened fur me that night, ah'll tell ye! Mind, ah wis only puttin it in cos Stevie hadnae had the chance yet."

Stevie's folded hands crept to the top of his head, the corners of his mouth inevitably following. "Ah'm sure ah would've goat aroond tae it eventually," he said drily.

"Aye. Aw-aw-aw ah'm sayin is, though, it's no somethin we can just hiv a wee bash at."

Ally nodded his head. "If a job's worth doing, it's worth doing well," he said brightly.

"Ah-ah-Ally's spot on." Robbie's glassy blue eyes floated fishily in his immobile rubber face. "Plus, if we get somebody in tae dae it an they make a mess o it, it'll no be oor problem."

Charlie furrowed his brow.

"Eh? Martin, you're the teacher. Is that right enough, it'll no be oor problem?"

Martin, startled, cast a quick look around. His features converged doubtfully towards the middle of his face.

"Ah'm an *English* teacher."

"Aye, but ye'll have read a book aboot it or sumthin, will ye no?" Charlie said.

Martin added his laugh to the general appreciative chuckle. "Well, ah'm nae expert, but in books an that folk can still go tae jail for attempted murder even if they just telt somebody else tae dae it fur them." He wrinkled his nose and loaded his 'Thoughtful' expression. "Probably you could get in trouble just fur bein here when we talked aboot it."

Ally's chair-legs made a scraping noise as he shot to his feet. "See ye later, boys!"

There was a fresh batch of chortling as Ally lowered himself into his seat, his forearm resting along the chair's back. Martin glanced up at   the clock.

164

"Right, look, we're obviously no gonnae dae it ourselves, so can we no bother wi the usual two-hour spiel aboot it? If we try tae dae it ourselves, it'll wind up wi aw *us* deid an Jimmy spendin the life insurance on tartan paint an watter wings for ducks."

Wullie laughed. "They'll no can tell the difference wi Stevie. He's half-deid as it is! Somebody haud a mirror up tae his face, the shock'll finish him aff."

Stevie's eyes crinkled with concealed merriment. "Don't you worry aboot me, boys, ah'm daein fine."

Charlie rumpled and unrumpled his agenda, significantly making a single oblique mark on it with an old biro. "Right, if we're aw agreed on that, we'll no need tae bother wae a vote. Does anybody know how much it costs?"

Ally nodded. "Aye, that's gonnae be the clincher. It's aw aboot money, in't it? Aw comes doon tae money."

"Ah-ah-ah've got a few pals'll know, mebbe even get ye a good price. Ah kin ask aroon, if ye like."

Charlie shook his head. "Naw, it's Stevie normally gets the quotes in, come tae think of it. Stevie, can we leave that wi you tae get a quote…"

165

"Three quotes!"

"Three quotes, an get back to us?"

Stevie forced his gummy eyes open only as wide as his thin-lipped smile. The irises, barely visible, slid into the corners of his eyelids. With an indistinct noise he adjusted his hands minutely behind his head.

Charlie glanced up at him with a little nod of satisfaction, then lowered his eyes to follow a tracing finger down the torn envelope.

"Right. Noo, aboot that pool table…"

At that there came the sudden rush of noise pouring into the room through a thousand tiny portholes; beeping and vibrating, cheery ring tones, staticky sound effects. They glanced at one another. Jackets were found, pockets emptied, screens switched on; and in the night, while the moles tunnelled patiently and the lawnmower turned to rust, into half-a-dozen private spaces came the half-a-dozen prophecies, "BAD NEWS…"

Not an Important Failure

"Jist bang it, son! *Hammer* it!"

Abruptly, as if hoping to catch it by surprise, Jamie pushes the clubhouse door back into its broken setting. For a moment there he holds it in Sisyphean poise before letting go, finger by finger, of the grubby alloy handle. The agonizing creak as it falls open again seems to drown out even the action on the pitch behind him. Pianos stop playing. Crows scatter.

"Naw, naw, naw," shouts one of the United faithful through a mouthful of pie, "Ye need tae *swing* it shut, pal! Gie it a guid hard swing!"

Prickling with the forty-something eyes of the United fans, Jamie slams the door shut hard. He is not surprised when it fails even to reach its setting, bouncing straight back off the frame and taking the skin off his knuckles. By now not only have the nearby punters turned completely round, but even the supporters on the far side of the ground are standing up and craning their necks for a better view. One of them, some twenty-odd yards away, cups his hands around his mouth and roars.

"IT'S COME AFF THE HINGES, MATE! YE NEED TAE LIFT IT UP!"

Jamie has already done this, but he knows that trying it again will be a lot less complicated and humiliating than explaining to the assembly why he isn't. He heaves upwards on the fragile handle whilst pushing the door back into place with his hip, then stands aside to let everyone see the door creep open again. By now almost no-one is watching the game, grateful instead for the distraction of Jamie's much more compelling and solvable problem. As he steps back to assess the situation, a man in a training jacket yells up at him.

"It's awright, pal, that's as far in as it goes. It willnae shut any mair than that."

A chorus of dismay and dissent breaks forth from all around. Jamie takes advantage of the momentary distraction to quietly shove the door back into place, praying for the sound of that wedging click. Instead, as he steps back, a wheezing, mocking groan, and another glimpse of the clubhouse toilets.

"Jiggle the handle, wee man!" somebody shouts.

"Gie the lock a gid thump!"

"Jist… jist leave it, son," slurs an old man, a bungee cord of saliva hanging from his beard.

The cacophony of suggestions gets louder and more excited, proponents of various schools of door-shutting thought bellowing up and down the stand at each other with the ardent seriousness of the righteous man. On the far side, even the Rovers fans are crying out their ideas with the relish of a sideshow barker. The United coach, arms perpetually folded, rotates on the spot to cast a disapproving glance up at the stands. Jamie stands there frozen, immobile, apparently forgotten in the joy of argument as first the history, then the genealogy of the door are dissected in terrifying detail.

"That door there's aulder than ma granda, never got fixed in aw its days!"

"Well, ah've been comin here man an boy for twenty-five years…"

"Aye, an ye look it! Ninety minutes ae this guff'd make onybody's hair faw oot!"

"Ah'm telling ye, that door never goat pit in until the Nineties! That wis when they pit in the fire escape!"

"Never! It wis Stevie Thorburn made that door, ah mind it masel…"

As the debate grows ever more inventive, the bartender, alerted by the alacrity of the crowd, sticks his head out the door. As it swings suddenly open, Jamie stumbles and nearly goes head-first down the stairs, reflecting (with some bitterness) that it is the only possible outcome from the situation in which he could hope to emerge with something like dignity. For a moment the barman's eyes follow the play with dim disappointment; then he disappears like a head from a port hole, slamming the door shut behind him.

Silence falls at the echoing thud. One by one, like sleepwalkers stumbling back into their lives, the fans shift round to watch the game. Jamie shuffles cautiously along the stand, stepping self-consciously over the crossed legs until he finds his seat. As he tries to stretch his arms out lazily, he is aware of how awkward and artificial his movement is, all of it, right down to the trembling of the minutest muscle. He is a composite, a machine of such complex mathematical and logistical equation as would baffle a watchmaker, an engineer. It is literally impossible that he can keep processing all the information that stops him from breaking down. And yet, he thinks, here he is.

Passing It On

It was never a good thing to be called to the manager's office, but to be shouted in an hour before a game? *That* was something else. In fact, it had been so long since Stevie Miller's last visit that he had forgotten what it was like to stand in front of that door, his hand raised pensively in mid-knock, his stomach discreetly devouring itself. As he rapped his knuckles decisively on the lintel - an old habit he'd never got out of – he noticed that, on the office door, the previous manager's name was still faintly visible through the paint. A decent fella, him. French, and maybe a bit too smart for his own good, but Stevie had liked him and been sorry to see him go. Then the hoarse voice came – *ENTER!* – and it was time, the door handle rattling loosely in his palm as an age-old scene unfolded before him; the plant pots, the desk; the gaffer looking up from nothing; the extended hand; the empty chair.

The very first time he had been called in to see the manager, he had only been a boy. For a laugh the other apprentices had told him he was getting the boot, and he had went straight home without a word, leaving the gaffer waiting. That might have been it for him and United, for him and football even, if the boss hadn't called that evening on his neighbour's phone. When he went in the next day, everyone was all smiles. The money they'd offered him to sign! At the time it seemed like riches. The other apprentices had been hanging around when he got out, lining up to shake his hand. He was loaded now, and they were waiting for him to buy them a drink. They were still waiting eight months later, when they were called into the office one by one and never seen again.

That was something he must have seen happen a few hundred times now, over the years, young boys and sometimes grown men emerging from the manager's office with red eyes and ashen faces. Sometimes you heard the door slam from the other side of the ground. Mostly, though, they went quietly, talking about their options, while the survivors joked and shook their hands and told them about all the other lads who'd been let go and come back again. There were at least two that Stevie could remember. It did happen.

Then Stevie became captain, and it was his responsibility to preside over these wakes. He did it well. For many youngsters it would be their last taste of professional football, and all they might have to show for it was that

Stevie Miller shook their hand and told them they could play. It was important they had that. And yet Stevie, if he was honest with himself, never really felt sorry for them. It was a terrible thing to say, but he actually kind of enjoyed it. They had caught a bullet that had once been meant for him, and deep down he was glad of it.

So when the manager called him in before the day's game, it had surprised at how little time the thing had taken. He'd expected there would be a lot to say, but it turned out that there wasn't. That afternoon, as they walked out of the tunnel, both teams, into the downpour of noise, Stevie noticed for the first time how much it was like the sky falling on you, this steep weight that rumbled down the stands and crushed whatever it fell on. Alone in the centre circle, he felt like a toy diver in a goldfish bowl, a plastic ornament pinned under water. Unnoticed but for a smattering of boos, John McAllister, the manager, crept past in his all-weather jacket, finding a seat in the dugout behind the subs. Stevie looked away. He was due a testimonial, McAllister'd told him – in the summer, maybe – but if he wanted to hang his boots up now, they'd see him alright. Otherwise, there were plenty of options; Hong Kong, America; maybe dropping down a league. If the right club came along, they'd be easy enough to deal with. It was the least he was due.

Stevie had digested all this uneasily, staring at the paperwork on the desk, before clearing his throat and saying that he'd rather stay and fight for his place at United. The gaffer had nodded and said he'd expected no less, but there was no admiration in his voice.

They kicked off. In the stands, the supporters chanted his name like usual. They didn't know. He raised his hand, and they cheered. He'd watched fellas drop down through the leagues from here, playing for less and less money in front of fewer and fewer people. He respected that, but it wasn't for him. He'd worked hard for this, and he wasn't about to give it up now, to end up playing on a park beside a cricket green. No. The only thing he could do now was to step it up a gear, make it difficult for the gaffer to get rid of him. If he could get back to how it was two seasons ago... Well, maybe *those* days were gone, but there was plenty of life in the old dog yet. And experience, that counted for something.

Yes, there was all that. He collected the ball, turned, played it on. He could kick on from here, earn his place back in the team. But then, hadn't he already earned his place? He'd given the best years of his life to this club, twenty of them. He didn't have to prove anything to anyone, never mind some wee guy whose name-paint was still fresh on the door. If the fans found out – if the *papers* found out – there'd be uproar. That boy's jacket was on a shoogly enough nail as it was. And as the idea came into Stevie Miller's head, his body prickled unpleasantly.

How many more games could he be, the gaffer, from the heavy dunt? Two, maybe? Three? The French lad got the heave-ho after finishing second, and they were fourth now. If they got beat today, that would surely be it. Was it, then, in the club's best interests that they win today, and risk McAllister being in the job another year? The ball whizzed past Stevie's foot as he stretched for it and missed. He wasn't saying he should throw the game – he wasn't saying that – but what reason did he have to try now, and whose fault would it be if he didn't? Everybody, even the youngsters, had go-slow periods in a game, chances to get their wind back or conserve their energy – well, what if he took one today, and it lasted ninety minutes? Who, if they knew the circumstances, would begrudge him that? Or even notice?

He shook off the idea and trotted back into position. Maybe they wouldn't notice. That was the worry. For the last few months, his right heel had been giving him some amount of trouble. It was daft to complain – who sat out for a sore heel? – but the pain had got so it was almost unbearable, a constant agony which throbbed straight through to the bone. He'd tried everything, tramadol, codeine, but nothing helped. If the gaffer hadn't expected so much from him, pressured him to play in every match, he might have come clean about it, taken an injection, missed a game. But the minute he gave up that shirt, he knew – he wasn't getting it back.

He limped around as best he could, but there was no question that the game was passing him by. When they came out for the second half it got worse, boys half his age coming on to brush him aside, shouldering into his heaving chest. He lurched at them, kicking after their heels, but it was hopeless. The play slunk further and further away, the ball a fading rumour, tortuously remote. His legs were gone, but his reading of the game, that was surely something he would never lose. Into the match's mystery he peered, and for a moment saw it, lucidly real – a pattern, the ball, and where it was going to go, and what he would have to do to win it. He set off.

***

As the ball skidded out crazily towards him, Andy Fowlis took a look over his shoulder. He'd only just made one decent run, and hadn't another one in him yet. If there was space to put his foot onto the ball, take a breath… There were seventy minutes gone and he felt as if he was gulping flames, the shallow gasps scarcely reaching his lungs before they were expelled again. It was all in his mind, of course, but once those fiery visions were fixed there in his head it was difficult to get them out. The nearest stand looked like a furnace to him, a giant bonfire that danced with flickering arms and crackled with fury. They'd been good with him, the United supporters, given him a round of applause during the warm-up and a cheer when the teams were read out. They remembered what he'd done for them, or at least what he'd tried to do. Nobody really ever appreciated you until you were gone.

It was a year now since he'd left. It'd been long expected, this business of the new broom, and when McAllister came in and talked about ends of eras, Andy had known that the jig was up. Still to be playing at 35 – that was a good innings. Most folk his age had long since called it a day.

But he hadn't been able to afford retirement then. There'd been bills to pay, and his wife not well. He'd prayed for help, and it had come, a year's contract at another club, and Eilidh, thank God, on the mend. But bad news, it didn't just come at pre-appointed times, waking you from sleep on bedside phones. It arrived whenever, and you had to be ready for it. It would be a while yet before he could think of hanging up his boots. And so there'd be another summer of hawking himself around, ringing friends and cold-calling grounds, hoping for a trial. The problems he'd had, most clubs knew about them. They didn't really care, but they knew about them. Anything that gave them the chance to hold out on you, to pull the offer back across the table and say *Well, if you think you can do better…* They were all over it. But at the time, when you were in that mess… everybody turned a blind eye, then. Nobody wanted to know.

No. There was no point dwelling on all that. People were doing their best for themselves, and his side of the street wasn't so tidy, either. He had taken honest inventory that morning, and admitted before himself and God that there was rage in his heart, and bitterness. It was wrong and unfair – a lot of good people had got down in the pit with him, and showed him the way – but it was how he felt. It was a human shortcoming, and he confessed it. But the satisfaction he had felt at the confession – was that not a shortcoming too?

There was a lot about the programme he didn't understand. It worked, no question, but it confused him. This business of giving yourself over to a higher power, for example. He didn't really believe in God, or Allah or whatever. But the sense that there was *something* there supporting him was definitely real. He'd searched everywhere for solutions - self-help manuals, Scientology, Buddhist cliques – but had so far come up with nothing. So what was this mysterious authority that had taken up his burden, and could it be wholly good? In Edinburgh, that free personality test had wound up costing him an arm and a leg… What if the whole thing was just a racket, a sort of spiritual Ponzi scheme, and the problems he thought he was passing on were piled up in some unseen corner, waiting to topple and bury him?

He mentioned these things to his sponsor, sometimes, a good man battling a miserable life; but the answers never helped. *Fake it till you make it.* That was the main one. *Don't look a gift horse in the mouth.* That was another. *If it ain't broke…* Maybe wisdom is just knowing the right cliché for the right occasion, Andy had thought. But then he had remembered his sponsor's son – killed, arbitrarily, by a brain aneurysm one day – and he'd changed his mind. Wisdom was whatever got you through the night.

The programme worked. Whatever his private misgivings about it, it worked. It was easy to forget now how bad things had been. People in groups like his, they could not help treating their pasts like picaresque anecdotes, ribald and essentially harmless. Who could blame them? Every story they had was just a moment away from tragedy.

Ye're no gittin in that car. No like that ye're no.

It had been Stevie who'd stopped him, wrestled for his keys. He hadn't been captain then, not yet – it was the big Norwegian lad then, the one who'd stood in the car-park and stared.

Ah'm fine. GET AFF ME!

And he'd swung at him with his fists, and struggled. The others, they'd passed on. Not Stevie.

Shh, it's awright, it's awright. Ye're comin hame with me, an it's awright.

Then he'd been sitting there in Stevie's living room, the kids playing round his feet, their mother watching him drink his tea. She smiled at him. On the hallway phone, a voice;

Aye, he's in a bad wey, like… Ah dunno… Two years, mebbe three? He's stertin tae sharpen up a bit noo. Ah'll bring him ower.

Stevie had never done the twelve steps himself, but he knew the score. He had picked Andy up from his door every morning, dropped him off in the afternoon. Weekends they had gone out together with their wives, the first sober friendships of Andy's life. It had been round about then that Eilidh had got sick – but even that circumstance had a normality to it which their lives had previously been devoid of. They had got through it with the help of many, and the fresh lease of life they had was tinged only with regret that they were starting again from so little.

After Eilidh's illness, there'd been hospital costs, private healthcare which he could then afford. It was different now. His salary was half now what it had been, and it would drop again next year, and keep dropping. Even that little money he was due was tied up in parameters and performances; appearance fees, win bonuses, cup runs. Everything he did out here on the pitch was either earning him money or costing him it. It was all part of the elegant scheme of sticks and carrots people rejoiced in imposing on those who'd made mistakes, and he would be living with it for the rest of his life.

He trapped the ball beneath his foot, rolled it back out with his sole. The other lads, their money was guaranteed. Victory, defeat, disaster, triumph; they'd laugh all the way to the bank. Andy alone needed to win, and he had a feeling today that it could be done. The boys in the home side had no appetite, and their fans were getting on their backs. Their gaffer's son, a spindly lad named McAllister, was getting it particularly bad. Andy strode into the opposition half, his eyes flashing everywhere for a run. Nothing was on, but another ten, fifteen yards and he would be in shooting distance himself; £250 a goal, £2000 on top for ten. He knocked the ball ahead, the space in front of him unfolding like a scene change in a theatre. It was there, coming, he *felt* it, and so could everyone around him; he knew already he was letting loose a peach, an unstoppable wallop into the postage stamp, a hush-gathering thunderball of a shot that would pull the net taut and threaten to uproot the trembling posts. He cut inside, neatly, with a glance at goal, took in and held his breath.

Then, suddenly, he was up in the air, his legs hacked away from under him. As he landed on his back the held breath burst from his lungs, a torrent of steam which gathered in the sky above his face. He grimaced and tried to get up. The base of his spine felt shattered, beyond all repair. It was a brutal challenge, cynical and stupid, and it had cost him the goal, the game, a few hundred pounds, maybe a few thousand. He took his time as he got up, dusting off his dirty knees and keeping his eyes down. The boy he'd been fouled by was standing there waiting, but he was in no hurry to look at him. He knew who it was.

Stevie Miller looked away, embarrassed. He thrust out his open hand. Andy stared. He looked at Stevie, who didn't look back, and shook his head.

"Nae need, Stevie," he said, "Jist nae need."

Stevie shrugged uncomfortably and walked away. The crowd booed, but it wasn't clear who or what. As his old teammate strolled off, Andy stood watching him, hands on hips, his breathing shallow and ragged. Something had gone badly wrong inside him, a broken thing that rattled round his chest like a bladder inside a ball, a pea inside a whistle. There was a free-kick to be taken, two hundred and fifty pounds worth, but that wasn't for him; he blasted the ball without thinking, lashed it straight at the nearest red shirt. Money was money, that was always true, but something else was walking away from him now.

***

Scott McAllister had noticed before how elastic time was in the vicinity of disaster. He remembered sitting in the back seat when his dad overtook, straining past lorries as the incoming traffic loomed. How slowly it all unfolded, the truck alongside creeping gradually into the past, the car in front an ominous blot spreading across the windscreen. Then, at the last moment, time would magically accelerate again, jumping into place like a stuck film suddenly unspooling, and it would all be over in a split-second of shouts and screeches, his dad screaming invective, his mother pale. And it was like that now, as Andy Fowlis kicked and the ball came off the ground towards him, moving so slowly Scott had time to notice every minute trembling of its path, its blue stitched panels shifting gently up and down. Sound hung frozen in the air, like heavy curtains untroubled by the wind, and in the final flourish of the swinging foot Scott read *agency*, clearly unfolding. These things happened, all the time – but the undeviating wickedness of that clubbing leg, its straightness perfect from knee to pointed toe, was no accident. The ball rose and rose, engulfing Scott's gaze like a world in fast approach, its myriad shadows throwing darkness everywhere, shadows Scott had been living in all his life.

His dad's career had been almost over by the time he was old enough to know. He could not recall having seen his dad play, except at training grounds, where gigantic men with stubbly chins glanced at him as they passed.

Zat yer boay, John? Awright wee man, whit's yer team?

And he'd press his burning face against his mother's palm, his hands squirming at his chest. Once, he'd burst out crying out when a kitman spoke to him. *Ah hope ye're a better finisher than yer da, son!* The man had smelled of drink, and Scott had been inconsolable. He had cried in the car the whole way home, while his dad and brother sat mortified up front.

Of the two of them, Craig had always been the player. *Disnae think aboot it too much,* their coaches would say as Scott sat listening on the bench, *Just keeps it nice and simple.* Dad had made them play in the same age group, even though Scott was two years younger. Mum didn't like it, but dad was adamant. *He needs tae toughen up, Maureen,* he'd say. *He's turning intae a right wee Mammy's boy.* Not that they spoke about him much, not until Craig had his accident. Afterwards, when the hospital switched off the machines and the kids sung a hymn at assembly, Scott spent more time with his father than he ever had before. His dad was coaching now, wee bits here and there wherever there was work – and there was always room in the youth team for Scott.

At training he worked hard and kept his head down, and on matchdays he was never on the bench, not for any longer than it took his dad to find out. His performances varied from inept to embarrassing, and on his worst days he could hear his dad groaning before he'd touched the ball. His teammates treated him with scorn, his coaches with contempt. But over time he got better – he couldn't not – and by the time his dad got his first post, and made Scott his first signing, he was able to hold his own. In the preceding years he hadn't made a single friend, or achieved anything else of note. All he had going for him was that he was John McAllister's boy.

As his father's ambitions took him from one club to another, Scott McAllister invariably went with him.

Rarely, if ever, did his previous clubs attempt to keep him after his father left. Whenever his dad was out of work Scott fell through the leagues like a stone, but it was never for long. John McAllister was the next big thing, and clubs were queuing up to make him offers, even if it meant taking on his son. When United made their move, Scott's contract with them had come in the same envelope as his dad's.

It had been a while in happening. When his dad had got wind that an offer might be imminent, he'd immediately handed in his notice at his current club, dusting off the old trope about "spending more time with his family". Scott had laughed when he'd read that. He, as usual, was immediately offloaded, free-transferred to an outfit five miles down the road. The facilities were poor and the money dreadful, but the coach was an old hand, an ex-miner from Kilwinning who knew the impossibility of enjoying things you hadn't earned. He treated Scott with respect, forced the young man to respect himself; and Scott, whose entire life had been lived through a sideshow mirror, both huge and tiny, crooked and straight – Scott, for the first time, gained the measure of himself. He had standards, attainable, and ambitions that were no longer sacrosanct but *real*, possible. They offered him a three year contract, and Scott signed without reading it. His dad had been furious. But when United phoned and said they wanted Scott McAllister, the directors hadn't asked for any money. *This is once-in-a-lifetime, Scott,* they'd said, and they slid his contract back across the desk. *We won't stand in your way.* On the last day, his teammates had covered his entire car with translucent red Post-It notes, United colours. Without removing them he'd got in and sat there in the terracotta light, listening as the others pulled away. His hands were locked tight to the steering wheel, his face in the mirror dead.

At his new club, it had been business as usual. He had hoped that he might be ready for it this time, able to earn his place in the team and keep it – but his failure's scale had been unprecedented, and even his father had been unable to prevent it. Like a millstone he had dragged his teammates down, their loathing of him politic and hushed, and by the time his father dropped him from the squad it was too late. The writing was on the wall for them both, and Scott's restoration to the team now was nothing more than a final act of defiance, a parting gift to the fifty thousand fans who mocked his runs and booed his every touch. As the

189

free-kick struck him in the face, he heard those boos turn suddenly to laughter, staccato barks which sounded like applause.

He spun clumsily as he fell, his hands reaching for his face, his body landing on its side. A sour tang of rust was in his mouth, and his eyes were spilling with tears. He scrambled to his knees and stopped, squeezing his nose's bridge, then reached down to steady himself, the cool wet feel of grass an unaccountable relief. For a long moment he crouched there and wished he had been knocked out, that he could wake up in hospital an hour from now and not remember. As he waited for the physio to come, Scott glanced up and realised that the game had not been stopped. No-one on either side had bothered to look at him, far less get him treatment. Crumpled by the pitch's side, he was nothing more than a comic sideshow, an embarrassing irrelevance. In the dugout, his father stared straight ahead, chewing gum. The only people who noticed as he struggled to his feet were the supporters in the nearest stand, who leaned across the barrier and jeered, their faces furious rims around their mouths. He recognised one, a window-cleaner who sometimes did his house, and always turned his hose off to say hello. He was bent double across the railing, roaring with laughter. Scott turned away and wiped his sleeve across his face. There was a dark streak along his arm.

Not knowing what else to do, he set off after the ball. Nobody was passing to him, or even looking at him. He wondered if his dad would sub him off. What a scene that would be. The crescendo, the catcalls, the sniggering rumble as he made his way off-field; a smaller city would be shaken into ruins. No, even his father knew better than that. Best to let things run their course, then slope off unacknowledged behind the rest.

Well, that would not be difficult. He had been sneaking all his life, hiding himself from one giant in the shadow of another. He'd spent his entire lunchtime once creeping behind an older kid at school, contorting his body to fit their shape as the bullies' stares scanned back and forth. After, their teacher had read them Anne Frank's diary. She had made it sound like something of a jape, a Blytonesque adventure with tea and scones. The Railway Children. But Scott had understood.

He stopped running. They were almost out of time. As the ball broke loose from a corner, it fell to someone in opposition blue, an elegant lad who looked casually over his shoulder and turned away without seeing him. *The invisible fucking man,* Scott thought to himself, and he broke into a sprint.

***

There was no reason for Danny to check the team-sheet before the games, but he always did it anyway. He had a good future ahead of him, he'd been told, if he kept his feet on the floor; and so every Saturday morning, as he got into the ground, he would pause for a moment at the groaning mass of tracksuits in front of the noticeboard, and elevate himself slightly up onto his toes for a look. The reserve team was written up in ink and difficult to read, but there it would always be, second from the top - *2. DANIEL SHIELDS*. But this morning had been different. The crowd around the corkboard had been thicker than usual, and when Danny had squinted through them at the team-sheet up the front he hadn't seen his name. Pushing his way closer to the board, his breath had caught in his chest, and his eyes started to hurt. Were they sending him back to the nineteens? He couldn't think of anything he'd done wrong. But there was no mistake; his name wasn't there, not even amongst the substitutes.

No you, son, someone nearby had said, *You're in the firsts.*

Danny froze. Everything inside him was struggling towards his head, like the bubbles of a lava lamp. His face was tingling, his ears crackled with blood, and his head bumped like a hot air balloon pulling against its moorings; but from the neck down he was nothing but a kind of sick emptiness, a taste of acrid rubber. *The firsts…*

They'd done this with him before, though. He maybe wasn't the smartest guy in the world, but he knew the kind of fun folk liked to have, especially when a young fella expects good things from life and is prepared to accept them without question. *Danny, there's a scout from Chelsea here to see you… Danny, that's The Sun on the phone, will I put them through?... Danny, the boss wants to see you in the car-park about a new contract…* And he never stopped falling for it because, really, he was more scared of missing out on a chance than he was of looking stupid. The only alternative was to live in the same world as the rest of them, where it was ridiculous that the Scotland manager would ever ring him up – and he wasn't ready for that.

He pushed his way over to the team-sheet for the first eleven. Sure enough, his name was there, right at the end. He glanced around, pulled out his mobile phone, and took a picture of it. Later, he'd put it up on Twitter and hashtag it something funny, maybe #alegendisborn or #thefirstofmany.

Hoi, Danny boy, first team bus is leaving in five!

Uncertainly, he picked up his bag and followed the first-team out into the car park. The boss was waiting for them. He shook Danny's hand and ushered him onto the bus, where the other players nodded at him over their phones. It was an hour's drive, and while his teammates checked their messages and listened to their iPods, Danny watched it all from his window seat with wonder, hearkening with rapt attention to every word they said. When they reached their opponent's ground, a clutch of home supporters were gathered outside, waiting to boo them; but Danny, oblivious, smiled and waved at them, and a couple waved back. Then they were there, on the surface of the pitch, passing it around as the stadium started to fill. Warming up in the other half were some of the greatest players in the country; when he'd skewed a pass in their direction, it had been Stevie Miller who'd returned it to him. *Stevie Miller*, who Danny'd been watching since he was a kid. He hoped that somebody had been filming it.

Once he'd taken his place in the dugout and the match had kicked off, Danny had focussed intensely on the action. The spectacle of it, the physical reality of the twenty-two men, subsumed the game as competition – to Danny it became absolute drama, a perfect sort of storytelling. By the time the stadium clock flashed into its last five minutes, and the manager told the substitutes to warm up, Danny wasn't even sure what the score was, or how to find out without looking daft. As he raced up and down the sidelines, alternating his sidesteps with sprints, he was arrested in mid-turn by a shout from the dugout, the manager's beckoning finger. He looked around. It was definitely him. Trotting back, his legs went suddenly weak, and he glanced up again at the stadium clock. There were two minutes left.

In the dugout he stripped off his tracksuit, the assistant manager gabbling frantically at him the whole while, like a salesman making a pitch through elevator doors. *Just keep it simple, Danny boy, nice and simple, easy ball every time…* He pulled his shirt on and shook off his freezing hands and then he was on the touchline, the fourth official fiddling with an electric display board, the referee with his notepad, scribbling something down. As the numbers went up and everybody on the field stared in interest, a blue shirt broke reluctantly from the pack and slowly jogged towards them.

"SUBSTITUTION FOR THE AWAY SIDE," the PA crackled flatly, "BEING REPLACED, NUMBER 2, ALEX PATTON, AND COMING ON, NUMBER 38, DANNY SHIELDS."

A small cheer from the away end filtered through the conversational buzz, and as Alex Patton slowed almost to a walk, holding his hand up in acknowledgement, Danny remembered seeing Stevie Miller make his Scotland debut in similar circumstances, in the dying minutes of a game gone moribund, to the polite applause of some scattered kids. Danny had been one of those kids. As he raced out onto the pitch and took up position, he tried hard not to wonder if this would be another such a moment, growing in significance as the years rolled by, like a boulder picking up moss.

The game restarted. As his defensive unit moved back and forth, Danny remembered with a pang that the match was almost over. Chances were that he would not even see the ball before the final whistle, never mind touch it. He prised his concentration from the task at hand and committed it to the psychic effort of willing the ball over in his direction. Just one kick would do, a crisp little pass, a header, anything at all that consummated his part in the game, made him a player rather than a spectator.

Then it came, the ball, breaking perfectly across the grass. He had time, and plenty of it; time to trap the ball and knock it on ahead, time to pick his head up and look into the void of green. Scott McAllister, who was supposed to be marking him, was nowhere to be seen. On the far left of the pitch, unseen by everyone, a winger was cutting into a thick wedge of room, his arm aloft. Anywhere in that vast sward and the ball was destined for the net. Danny stepped forward into the pass, shaping his body to the swing of his right foot, and visualised (as he always did) the arc of the speeding ball, motionless in the air as the Earth moved obediently around it.

As his foot reached the top of its backswing, it caught on something coming in behind him, something supple and hard and moving fast, and the entire mechanism of his body, calibrated around the curve of that boot, shook and fell to pieces. Danny hit the floor with a graceless crash, imagining the sound of nuts and bolts scattering everywhere, tiny pieces of his earlier vision rolling into the pitchside gutter and skittering unseen in the grass.

Suddenly he could not breathe, the last, controlled intake of air trapped in his chest, an oesophageal logjam of breath going in and breath going out, and he writhed on the dirt in panic, his knees pulling up to his chest, his hands clawing desperately at the ground.

Stop the game! Ref! Ref!

A hand was on his arm, another fluttering over his head like a bird. Someone shouted for help; his vision started to run like a painting, a wall of muted colour without shapes. Then there was the smell – it kicked him in the chest, and he lurched up from out of himself, gasping for air.

Easy, wee man, easy.

Somehow he was on his feet, the physio helping him off the field. Behind them, the game resumed and then abruptly ended. The crowd began to disappear. Players funnelled quickly towards the tunnel, shaking hands and occasionally swapping shirts – dizzily, Danny remembered about Stevie Miller, but he could not see him.

As the physio collected his bags, Danny shuffled along the touchline, head down, like a man looking for change. Piece by piece he picked them up and reconstructed them, the moments of the past. He saw himself in textbook poise, foot drawn back, arms cast out in symmetry; then rolling comically on the floor in front of fifty thousand people, drowning in his own fear. Some debut that was to remember. Some moment that had been.

He reached the end. The stadium was almost empty, just a few long columns of red passing through as they talked about something else. Stewards were sweeping up, lumps of tin foil bouncing down the steep stairs, programmes abandoned everywhere. Next to the tunnel, a small boy in a blue hat leaned over the fence, stretching his arm out as far as he could. Danny turned his face away, his eyes full. He did not see that the hand was meant for him, and the silken sleeve of his shirt passed through it like water.

Acknowledgements

The following stories and poems were first published and/or broadcast elsewhere. Thanks and acknowledgements are due for:

Take Shelter and *The Timin o the Run*, which were first published in *The Scotsman*.

The Battle o Philiphaugh, which was written for and broadcast by BBC Radio Scotland.

Team Photo: Selkirk, 1946, which was written for and broadcast by BBC World Service.

Five Hunner Miles (Away tae Nairn), which was written for and broadcast by Sky Sports News.

A Stranger Here Myself and *The River of Silver*, which were first published in *The Eildon Tree*.

Slave Labour, which was first published in *The Crazy Oik*.

The Eye of the Needle, which was first published in *Pushing Out The Boat*.

Auld Airchie's Losin It, which was first published in *McStorytellers*.

Bad News, which was first published in the New Voices Press anthology *Making Waves*.

Scatter My Ashes at Claggan Park, which was first published in the Derby QUAD anthology *Offside Stories*.

Thanks to Sara Clark, Duncan Taylor, David Hendry and Simon Malone for their helpful feedback on the various pieces contained within this collection. To my family as well for their continual support, and particularly Elizabeth Granger, Slim Belkadi, Jayne Belkadi, Roisin Stewart and Alex Law. And to the various kind-hearted people who have unwittingly encouraged me in my scribbling: Gail Hendry, Karen Hendry, Carol Douglas, Calum Kerr, Paul Wheelhouse, Bob Dickson, Ian McMillan, Rab Wilson and Matthew Fitt.

Thanks also to the Borders football mafia, and especially John Slorance, Jason Marshall, David Knox, Dave Scott, the good folks at Nil By Mouth, and everybody at my old club, Hawick Royal Albert.

The local arts scene has been a continual source of inspiration and encouragement. Amongst many others, Jules Horne, Dorothy Alexander, Alastair Redpath, Bridget Khursheed, Mary

Morrison, Richard Ashrowan and Bridie Ashrowan have contributed massively to the creation of our flourishing creative community. Further afield, Stephen Watt and Jim Mackintosh have made writing about football seem like a relatively sensible thing to do, as have my teammates at the Scotland Writers Football Team.

Particular thanks to the committee, players, and coaches of Selkirk Football Club, and especially to Ross Anderson, Drew Ketchen, Sheree Davison, Keith Wilson, Steve Forrest and Garry O'Connor.

And most of all, thanks to the supporters, of Selkirk FC and of every other club. Except Gala Fairydean.

Oh, alright. Even the Fairydean.

About the Author

Thomas Clark is a poet, writer and freelance journalist. In 2015, he was appointed Scottish football's first ever poet-in-residence, taking up a position with Lowland League side Selkirk FC. Thomas's work has been published in The Scotsman, The Sunday Mail and Bella Caledonia, and broadcast on ITV, BBC and Sky Sports.

His 2015 poetry collection "Intae the Snaw" was praised by poet Rab Wilson as "an important collection that timeously re-establishes the power, virr an smeddum o the Scots language" and by writer Matthew Fitt as "Brilliant… Tammas Clark taks the bonnie broukit bairn that is Scots an blaws new life intae the hail clamjamfrie".

He blogs at www.thomasjclark.co.uk, and can also be found on Twitter @ClashCityClarky

Printed in Great Britain
by Amazon